The Call of the Tide

Joe Vasicek

Other books by Joe Vasicek:

The Widow's Child
The Unknown Sea
Rescuer's Reward
The Call of the Tide
The Winds of Desolation
Bloodfire Legacy

Genesis Earth
Edenfall
The Stars of Redemption

Queen of the Falconstar
Captive of the Falconstar
Lord of the Falconstar

Star Wanderers
Children of the Starry Sea
Return of the Starborn Son

Bringing Stella Home
Desert Stars
Stars of Blood and Glory
Heart of the Nebula

The Call of the Tide

Joe Vasicek

CONTENTS

For Piper.

HTTL

In Which I Face Humiliating Rejection and Fall Unwittingly Into a Trap

Call me Samuel—or really, whatever you like. I've been called a lot of things, some better, some worse. It's the hair. Outside of a desert isle, you don't often see a man with hair this shaggy—at least, not in the merchant kingdom of Caravelia.

If it weren't for my magic, I never would have grown my hair out like this. But as fate would have it, that seems to be the only way I can actually use my magic. Keeping my hair clean is difficult, since combing tends to pull out strands, and since tying it back gives me this awful tingly feeling all over my scalp, I prefer to wear it free. And of course, cutting is out of the question.

It's not easy being a shaggy-haired sea mage in a kingdom where most men keep their hair neat and trimmed. But on this particular day, I was feeling pretty good about life. I'd bought some new clothes and spent the whole morning cleaning my hair, so I felt refreshed and confident as I strode down the bustling cobblestone streets toward the harbor. The last few months had been rough, but I was sure that this would be the day I'd sign on with a new crew.

Now, most sea mages have no problem finding a captain to sign them. Magical gifts aren't particularly rare, but they are uncommon. And an experienced mage can usually write his own ticket on a ship just as well as a skilled blacksmith on land. Unfortunately, my hair wasn't my only hurdle. I'd also dropped out from the King's Fleet, making me something of a pariah. (It's a long story, and I don't really care to tell it right now.)

To mitigate some of that sting, though, I carried a letter of recommendation from my best friend and former captain, Sir Jason Callidor. Jason and I went back a long way, to the time before he'd become a lord and knight of the realm. Our paths had parted—a man has to stand on his own eventually, after all—but the letter put a bounce in my step that otherwise would not have been there.

So I strode confidently toward the harbor, taking in the sights and sounds of the bustling marketplace. The cobblestones were slick from recent rain, though the sun now shone brightly in a blue summer sky. Vibrant stalls lined the narrow thoroughfare, overflowing with colorful spices, delicious fruits, and freshly caught seafood, the air thick with their mingled scents. Merchants vied loudly for attention from the bustling crowd, while heavy-laden donkeys brayed in protest. In short, it was a day like any other in the port city of Caravelia, lovely in all its colorful chaos.

As I stepped onto the docks, I could feel the weight of disapproving eyes on me, but it didn't bother me in the slightest. I walked to the end of the pier and stopped, admiring the ship before me. She cut an impressive sight—blue-and-white sails and a gold-gilded hull tapering smoothly to the bow, where a beautiful carving of a flaxen-haired woman leaned proudly into the waves. A bell chimed from the deck, calling her crew. Oh, how I longed to join them!

The captain, a grizzled old veteran with short-cropped wavy hair, eyed me suspiciously from the aftcastle as I approached. It seemed a long shot that he'd have me, but I would be damned if I let an opportunity like this slip through my fingers.

"Ahoy!" I called, waving to him. "Quite the beauty you have there."

"May I help you?"

The quartermaster, a thoroughly bald man with beady eyes and a bulging belly, had already moved to intercept me. I could tell that he was eager for an excuse to send me away. Undeterred, I smiled and offered my hand.

"The name's Samuel Cox. I'm a sea mage, looking for a ship to sign onto. I assure you, I'm one of the best."

His scowl deepened. "Do you come with any letters, lad?"

"Of course." I handed him the parchment, which he slowly unrolled.

"'Sir Jason Callidor,'" he muttered after reading through it. "Isn't he that young freelancer who was knighted after the Valinarian affair?"

"The very same."

He grunted and rolled up the letter. "He never was much of a merchant. Always up to his eyeballs in debt, as I recall."

My smile became strained, but I kept my eyes locked on his, determined to make a good impression. Unfortunately, a small bird chose that very moment to alight on top of my head, probably mistaking my hair for a bush. I hesitated for a moment, unsure whether to brush it away. I decided against it. After all, I didn't want to make a scene.

"I sailed with him for many years, sir," I told the man. "In fact, it was largely due to my skills that—"

"Yes, yes. Who did you sail with before that?"

My stomach fell. Telling the truth might sink my chances, but there was no other way around it. My time in the King's Fleet was a matter of public record and easy to check.

"I sailed with His Majesty's fleet for a time," I explained hesitantly. "But my service there... ended prematurely."

"Oh? And why was that?"

"I dropped out, sir."

The quartermaster studied me, his eyes narrowing. The bird chose that moment to fly away, but its foot got caught in my hair. Unable to escape, the creature flopped against the side of my face, chirping angrily. I tried to brush it away as casually as I could manage.

"You're not one of those kooky followers of the New Ways, are you?"

"Are you talking about my hair, sir? I wear it out like this because of my magical gifts. If I were to cut it, I would lose my powers."

He grunted again and handed me back the letter. "Be that as it may, we have no need of your services, Master Cox. Good day to you."

At that moment, I felt something warm and wet run down my ear. The stupid bird had chosen that moment to crap on me. I walked a short distance away before knocking it out of my hair, ducking as it angrily circled a few times before finally flying off. Then, reaching into my vest pocket, I withdrew a handkerchief and cleaned up the mess.

As I walked back down the bustling dockside street, I caught a glimpse of my reflection in a nearby window. My hair, wild and untamed, stood out amongst the more neatly groomed sailors around me. Would it really hurt that much to cut my hair and join them, denying my gifts? With a few quick snips, I would become just another mediocre sailor—but at least I would belong.

A bell tolled, breaking me out of my melancholy thoughts. I caught a whiff of freshly baked bread from a nearby bakery, which did much to lift my spirits. Hot, fresh bread may seem like simple peasants' fare, but we rarely have it on the high seas. My mouth began to water in anticipation, and I reached for my money pouch to count my coins.

It was then that I noticed a glint in the window behind my reflection. An old, weather-beaten compass sat amidst a shelf of curiosities in the display. Its brass casing was scratched and battered but polished to a high shine. I paused, strangely drawn to it. If only I could find my own life's direction so easily...

"Fine instrument, that," the merchant noted from the doorway. "Would you like to hold her?"

"Yes, sir," I said, nodding my thanks.

The merchant went inside to retrieve it, coming out a few moments later. I ran my fingers over the intricate engravings, admiring its weight and craftsmanship.

"Solid piece—they don't make it like this anymore."

"Aye," I said softly. "Have you had it for very long?"

The merchant shrugged. "About a year, give or take. Got it from a pawnbroker. It's such a fine piece, I thought it would have sold by now. But most people judge by outward appearances, and don't take the time to recognize true worth."

I nodded, suddenly feeling a sense of kinship with the instrument. It had a thin chain, for hanging around one's neck. I already wore an old scrimshaw locket under my shirt, a memento of my mother passed down to me from my father, but a compass like this one wouldn't hurt. Could I justify the expense, though? My money purse had grown awfully light.

"Here," said the merchant, taking it to show me something. He opened the case, and I saw that the stone on which the needle rested had some mildly magical properties.

"Is that a scrystone?" I asked.

"Aye," the merchant answered. "The craftsman who fashioned this piece had the gift."

I smiled. The scrystone made the piece much more than a simple compass. Even without the gift of magic, a man could use a stone like that to catch glimpses of his future or to find lost things. As a skilled mage, I had little need for such an aid, but a stone like that could still have its uses.

"How much?" I asked.

The merchant scrunched his eyes. "Normally, I'd ask thirty coppers for a piece like this. But you seem like a decent fellow, and it does need a home." He paused for a moment, then declared, "Ten coppers."

Ten coppers! At that price, it was an absolute steal, but I frowned in spite of my excitement. Was this merchant trying to be charitable? Or was he a follower of the New Ways, and had recognized me as one, too? No matter. I wasn't about to let an opportunity like this pass me by.

As I left the shop, I slipped the compass around my neck, next to my scrimshaw locket. The brass and the ivory made a pleasant clinking sound as I walked. I reached under my shirt for the compass, holding it in hand—

—and suddenly, I had a vision of a dozen cloaked and hooded figures surrounded by dripping candles, chanting in unison. It lasted only an instant, but my mind focused on one in particular: a young woman with dark red hair. I could feel her fear, but she'd lived with it for so long that she'd hardly known anything else. And though she was one of them, I felt very strongly that she was not supposed to be there.

Someone bumped my shoulder from behind, bringing me back to the present. "Stop blocking traffic, you vagrant!" he snapped before moving on.

I stepped to the side of the street and pondered what I had just seen. That girl—something about her seemed familiar. What had she been doing in that eerie place? Did she need to be rescued? It seemed that she was there against her will, though in my vision, she had clearly been a participant in that dark, arcane ritual.

Closing my eyes and clutching the scrystone to my chest, I reached out with my magic, searching for her. She was not in Caravelia, I was sure of that. Somewhere over the sea, perhaps? I felt a faint tug toward the south, but I couldn't sense anything more. The scrystone, having briefly shown her to me, was now suddenly silent.

If she was over the sea, I had no chance of finding her unless I signed on with a ship. So I took a deep breath and tried to use the scrystone again.

"Take me to the best ship to sign on with," I whispered, shutting all else from my mind. Once again, the scrystone gave me a picture, this time of a gold-trimmed caravel preparing to set sail. The crew scurried about the decks, their urgent movements signaling a need for more skilled hands. With the scrystone, I sensed that they hadn't yet signed a mage.

I hurried down to the dock, arriving just before they lifted the gangway. "Ahoy there!" I called. A burly old sailor with dark black hair peered down at me from the shroud.

"What do you want, stranger?"

"I'm an experienced sea mage, looking for a berth. You seem to be needing extra hands."

The sailor frowned skeptically, eyeing my hair. "The captain don't take just anyone. You'll have to speak with her directly. Come."

I eagerly strode across the plank and met the sailor as he climbed down the rigging to join me. He grunted and shook my hand, turning to indicate the cabin. The captain stepped out of the doorway, frowning as she saw me approach.

"Who's this, Jim?" she asked, locking eyes with me. She was a formidable woman, with fiery red hair and piercing green eyes. She stood tall, with her hands on her hips. Her gaze swept over me with a critical eye.

"My name's Samuel Cox, ma'am," I said, smiling as I extended a hand. "I couldn't help but notice that you seem a bit shorthanded. I'm an experienced sea mage, currently looking for a ship like yours to sign on with."

My words hung awkwardly in the air as she eyed me up and down. "You don't look like much," she said gruffly.

"I have a letter of recommendation," I said, handing it out to her. "From Sir Jason Callidor, knight of the realm."

She took it, glanced over it briefly, then handed it back, her expression unchanged. My heart sank.

"He was my last captain. I served under him faithfully for years."

"And before?"

"The King's Fleet," I admitted. "But I left that career to follow my own path."

"Dropped out, eh?"

My breath caught in my throat. In my mind's eye, I once again saw the shame on my father's face when I told him I'd left the King's Fleet. The bitter taste of failure flooded my mouth, and I tried in vain to exude a sense of self-confidence that I barely felt.

"Cut your hair," she commanded. "If you do that, we'll have you."

My throat tightened. "With respect, ma'am, you don't know what you're asking. My magic—"

"If you need to keep it long like a savage to cast your spells, I won't have you. I keep a tight ship here, and I won't stand for breaches of discipline—particularly not from a dropout like you."

Her words stung like a whip, but I refused to be cowed.

"Captain," I pleaded, meeting her sharp eyes. "I may not look like much, but I know how to work hard. I won't disappoint you. Please, give me a chance to prove myself."

"Didn't you hear what I said, lad? You're not fit for the job. Now off with you, before I have you thrown off!"

The dockhands were already starting to cast off as I scurried back across the gangway. The sailors pulled it up, and the ship's sails filled slowly with wind as the ship backed away. I stood there on the dock, watching forlornly. Had the scrystone led me astray? Or was this truly the best I could hope for?

My spirits, which had flown so high before, now felt utterly crushed. More than ever, I longed to be back at sea, where the salty wind tossed my shaggy mane, far from the judging eyes of my more conservative countrymen. Also, the girl from the vision haunted me. I felt that I had to find her somehow, but without a berth, how could I?

Listless and discouraged after a long and exhausting day, I trudged up the street from the harbor. After so much rejection, it was hard not to feel defeated and depressed. As the sun dipped under the sea, it also seemed to be setting on my future. After all, if my best hope for a berth had rejected me, what sort of future did I have?

The mouth-watering scent of stew and fresh bread pierced my gloomy thoughts. How long had it been since I'd eaten? Far too long. Though money was tight, I followed the magnificent scent to a nearby tavern, reasoning that I would get more benefit from a good, warm meal than from pinching a few precious coppers.

The tavern was alive with laughter and boisterous conversation. Sailors, merchants, and skilled craftsmen had all gathered to relax at the end of another day. A grimmer crowd more to my own state of mind would come later, drinking their sorrows into oblivion, but for now the place was lively and warm.

"A bowl of stew and a tankard of ale," I told the barkeep, laying down a few coppers. He nodded and came back with a steaming bowl and a tall pewter mug. The hot, meaty stew was exactly what I needed, and I ate eagerly, the cheap ale chasing it down like ambrosia.

"What's got you troubled, lad?" the barkeep asked.

I sighed. "Just another luckless day, I suppose."

"In life or in love?"

"Just life, I suppose," I told him. "I've been looking for a ship, but none will take me. I suppose it's the hair."

The barkeep quirked an inquisitive eyebrow at me. "New Ways, is it?"

"Something like that," I said carefully.

"Don't you worry, lad. We're friendly to all in this establishment. Times may be changing, but everyone's welcome here so long as they've got coin."

"Thank you, sir," I answered, relieved to hear it. The barkeep wandered off to take care of another customer, and I settled down to nurse my drink in solitude.

"Had a tough run of it, eh?" a low, gravelly voice came in my ear.

I turned to face the speaker, a grizzled old sea dog with one milky eye and a bushy beard. "You could say that," I mumbled, not really wanting to engage.

"They don't like the looks of ya, do they?" he continued, oblivious. "The hair, I mean," he added, stabbing a gnarled finger toward my head.

I sighed. "It is a curse sometimes."

"I've seen many a man like you with dreams in his eyes and magic in his veins, only to be turned away because of some such nonsense." His good eye twinkled at me. "But I've got some good news for you: a lead on a ship needing a mage with... special talents."

I perked up, suddenly interested. "Where can I find this ship?"

"I can take you there now, if you like. But I warn you, it won't be easy. The captain is a tough one, and he doesn't suffer fools lightly. If that don't bother you, though..."

A short while later, I found myself in the shadows of an alley, where the stench of refuse mingled with the briny scent of the sea. My weathered companion from the tavern emerged from the shadows, a crooked smile splitting his ugly face.

"Follow me, lad, and mind yer step."

Without hesitation, I followed him down the darkened way. The night air was cool and crisp, and our footsteps echoed off the high, dark walls around us. Despite our shady surroundings, I felt a sense of excitement and anticipation. After all, this was just the sort of lucky break I'd been wishing for.

As we turned down a side street, a sudden sense of unease pierced my blind euphoria. The neighborhood we walked into was seedier, with decayed and abandoned door fronts lit only by the pale moonlight. Shadows danced around us as we delved deeper into the darkness.

"Just how much farther exactly?" I asked. We seemed to be going downhill toward the harbor, but the twisting side streets had turned me around so much that I wasn't sure where we were.

"Not far now, lad," the man said. His words did little to lift my growing unease.

Finally, we turned into a dim and empty courtyard. My sense of foreboding spiked, but before I could say anything, a tall figure emerged, clad in dark robes. His face was obscured by a deep cowl, but his mere presence exuded power. A half-dozen other hooded figures stood behind him, much like the vision I'd seen in the scrystone compass.

A chill ran down my spine. Had I blundered into a trap?

"Well done, Balthazar," the tall man said, his voice dangerously smooth. He pulled back his cowl to reveal an angular, mustached face, with raven-black hair cut short and eyes like shards of ice. My breath caught in my throat as his eyes met mine.

"We have much to discuss, you and I," he said softly.

I turned to run, but more figures emerged from the shadows behind me, their upraised hands already glowing with an unearthly light. I felt a surge of power as their dark spells fell upon me, and suddenly I was unable to move. Someone pulled a hood over my head and everything went black.

In Which I First Glimpse the Tidecaller's Amulet and Flee to an Old Friend

I felt a moan escape my lips as I came back to my senses. My head spun, and I felt as if I'd been kicked by a horse—or worse, by a burst of dark magic. Which, in this case, happened to be true.

I forced my eyes open and blinked them clear. I was seated in a dank and windowless room, cool like a root cellar, illuminated only by flickering candles. Lots of candles. And yet, for all that flame, they seemed to do little to dispel the cold or the darkness.

Dark magic, then. It had to be. But the subtle scent of salt and brine told me I wasn't far from the harbor.

As my awareness slowly returned, the shadows seemed to press against me, enclosing me in their cold embrace. I then noticed the giant chalk circle and arcane symbols scrawled around me on the floor. The chair I was bound to sat in the center of the circle, surrounded by more than a dozen hooded cultists, their faces and figures cloaked.

The sight of them filled me with shock that I hadn't seen them before. "What do you want?" I asked defiantly.

They refused to answer, their faces shrouded in shadow. It was clear enough that I was part of some twisted ritual. Was I to be sacrificed, then? I tried to pull my hands free, but I was held in place by more than physical cords.

A man stepped forward and pulled back his hood, and I recognized him at once as their leader. In the eerie candlelight, I could see that he kept his jet-black beard trimmed in one of the newer styles, a pointed goatee with an unconnected mustache. He had high, sharp cheekbones and deeply sunken eyes.

"Welcome, Samuel," he said, his voice both chilling and smooth. "I've been looking forward to this meeting for some time."

"Who are you?"

"I am called Malachai. That is the only name you need know."

"What do you want with me? Why am I here?"

He smiled humorlessly. "Because of who you are—and more importantly, what you can become."

I struggled in vain against the spells that bound me. Surrounded by the hooded cultists, I felt all but helpless beneath Malachai's predatory gaze.

"I don't know what you're talking about."

"Oh, you will," Malachai assured me. "But first, where is the amulet?"

I frowned. "The amulet?"

"Yes. The Tidecaller's Amulet. I suspect it lives on in your family legend, a story handed down to you through the generations."

"I've never heard of any such thing."

"Don't play dumb with me, Samuel," Malachai commanded, his smile quickly turning to a sneer. "I know of the powers that you possess, even if you do not."

My mind raced as I looked for a way out of this precarious situation. But something about Malachai's words reverberated within me, igniting a flickering flame of curiosity that quickly began to flare.

"I swear, I have no idea what you're talking about."

Malachai loomed closer, his malevolent aura sending chills down my spine. His eyes glinted in the candlelight as he spoke.

"Then allow me to jog your memory. Your... *ancestral* memory."

He put his hand on my shoulder. A sharp pain jolted through my skull, causing me to cry out in agony. My vision blurred—and suddenly, vivid images began to bombard me: epic sea battles raging under darkened skies, colossal ships clashing with thunderous force, and a powerful amulet hanging around my neck, pulsing with untapped energy.

As the pain dissipates, a torrent of knowledge floods my mind. I see myself standing tall on the deck of a ship, wielding the full power of the amulet against my foes. Adrenaline surges through my veins as I summon a mighty monster from the deep, one who has not arisen since the founding of the world. He is mine to command, as are the very elements—the wind, the waves, and the tides.

But that is just the beginning. The visions continue to pour into my mind, pulling me ever deeper. I navigate treacherous waters, face perilous foes, and uncover ancient secrets that were long forgotten before man ever dared to sail the seas. The intensity of it all threatens to blind me. But amidst the chaos, there is also a thrilling sense of adventure. For I know that I am destined for greatness—to rule not only the tides, but everything touched by them.

Malachai released his grip on my shoulders, and the vision ended as abruptly as it had come, leaving me gasping for breath. The last thing I saw before the vision fully faded was a jungle island somewhere in the tropics. But my head was still swimming with so many images that I hardly knew what to make of it.

"Do you comprehend it now, Samuel?" Malachai hissed. "You are the chosen one, destined to wield a power that the world has not seen since the passing of the age of legends."

Even as he spoke the words, I realized that there was truth in them—though how much, I did not know. Something about that vision had touched the deepest part of my soul, and deep down, I knew there was no turning back from what I had felt and seen.

I blinked and pictured the amulet—a dark, round stone set in a silver pendant. Something about that image filled me with a sense of power strong enough to break the cords and binding spells that held me. For the moment, however, I held myself back.

"Do not resist your destiny," Malachai said, his voice taking on a hypnotic tone. "With the amulet, your power will be unimaginable."

The cultists tightened the circle. I could feel their fanatical devotion as they began to chant in unison, their voices slowly rising to a crescendo. At that moment, I knew I had to get out of there.

I clenched my fists and gritted my teeth, calling on the vision of the amulet. My body trembled with effort, weakening under the assault of the cultists' chant.

With a loud crack, the suddenly spell shattered and the chair broke into pieces beneath me. I fell to the ground in a heap.

Before the cultists could react, I sprang to my feet and summoned a blast of wind. Even within the cellar, my powers served me well. The furious gust knocked the cultists aside, opening a path for my escape.

"Stop him!" Malachai roared.

Without thinking, I charged through the door and climbed a flight of stairs into a dark alleyway. The cultists' shouts sounded behind me as I dashed into the shadows, heedless of where I ran.

After seeing the vision of the amulet, everything had changed. Not only had it awoken an unknown power within me, aiding my escape, but it had filled my mind with knowledge. And yet, so many questions remained. The amulet had been lost for centuries, but my fate was tied to it—indeed, it always had been—in ways that I barely understood. And until I held that amulet in my hands, my newfound powers were only a fraction of what they could be.

All of those thoughts were relegated to the back of my mind, however, as my primary objective in that moment was simply to escape. I ran down the nearly empty streets, my unkempt hair whipping behind me as I dodged sleeping drunks and dozing beggars. Unless I found some refuge, the cultists were certain to find me, and I doubted I would be able to get away again.

My thoughts suddenly turned to Jason Callidor, my old friend and captain. Our ways had only parted because he'd given up the seafaring life for the court, discharging his new responsibilities with his royal-born wife. They lived in a grand estate overlooking the harbor.

I turned that direction, praying inwardly that Jason was home. He had told me that I was welcome, but I was still worried that his servants might see my shaggy hair and turn me away like some common vagrant. But I put those worries out of my mind as I ran up to the iron gates of the estate.

"Help!" I shouted, pounding on them. "Jason! Are you there? Help me!"

After nearly a minute, a candle appeared in the window, and the front doors opened. A clean-shaven man with tousled, dirty-blond hair stepped out. The rest of the household must have been asleep.

"Jason!" I said, relieved to see it was him. He looked at me and frowned.

"Samuel?"

"Yes, it's me. Please—let me in!"

He hurried to the gate and swung it open. "What's going on? What manner of devilry chases you tonight?"

"It's madness, Jason. Sheer madness. I was kidnapped by some sort of cult, led by a dark sorcerer. I barely managed to escape."

Jason glanced down the road outside before carefully shutting and barring the iron gate. "You're safe now. Come inside and tell me everything."

I followed him into the foyer of his house, taking in the grandeur of the place. Intricate tapestries adorned the walls while exotic rugs covered the tile underfoot. Jason led me down the hall through another set of ornately carved doors and into a spacious room lined with bookshelves. I collapsed onto an overstuffed divan. The place was so luxurious that even in my new suit of clothes, I felt out of place. Not that it mattered a whit to my friend. Jason and I had been through so much together that his presence alone did much to set me at ease.

"Now, why don't you tell me what's going on," Jason said.

I took a deep breath and ran a hand through my hair. "I was just getting supper at a tavern, lamenting not being able to find a ship to sign on with, when this old man told me he might know a captain in need of a sea mage. He led me to an alleyway where a dark sorcerer named Malachai kidnapped me. He took me to some cellar hideout and tried to induct me into his cult!"

"A cult, you say?" Jason asked, frowning.

"Yes. They're after a powerful artifact known as the Tidecaller's Amulet. Malachai bound me with his magic and showed me a vision of it." I paused, thinking through things clearly for the first time. "He said that only I can wield the amulet, which is why he wanted to bring me under his sway. I think it has something to do with my hair."

"The source of your magic," Jason mused.

I nodded and recounted every chilling detail of my encounter with the cult, from their dark robes and eerie auras to the magic circle they had drawn on the floor. "I barely made it out of there alive," I finished, my voice trembling.

"That is concerning," said Jason, stroking his chin. "And you didn't see any of their faces, except for Malachai's?"

"No."

Jason grunted. "A cult of dark magic, hidden among us. Anyone in the city could secretly be one of them."

"Except you, I hope," I said, smiling weakly at my joke.

He laughed good-naturedly. "Yes—except me. You did the right thing, coming here. You can always trust me."

"I know," I said quickly, "but whom else can we trust? I can't stay in your estate forever, and it won't take them long to find out where I've gone."

The opening of a door interrupted our conversation, and Lady Julietta strode in. Jason's wife was as elegant as ever. Her long auburn hair cascaded down her back, glinting ever so subtly in the warm candlelight. Her piercing blue eyes reminded me of the sea. Framed with long lashes, they seemed to hold a wisdom beyond her years. Even though it was late in the evening, she wore a regal blue gown, adorned with delicate lace that traced intricate patterns across the fabric. A gold belt was cinched at her narrow waist, adding to her striking appearance.

"Samuel," she said, gliding gracefully across the room. "What troubles you?"

"A dark sorcerer and a secret cult," Jason explained on my behalf. "They're led by a man whose name is Malachai, and he wants to bring Samuel under his sway."

Julietta frowned. "Truly?"

I nodded and told her everything. Her expression remained cool, though I could tell her mind was racing. When I explained the powers of the amulet, her lips narrowed.

"Do you believe this amulet truly possesses such power?"

"Yes," I told her, drawing a long breath. "I didn't just see its power in that vision—I *felt* it. I *used* it, to escape."

"Then it seems to me that the amulet is the key," Julietta said, looking at us both. "We must act swiftly to find it and destroy it."

Jason and I both frowned. "Destroy it?"

"Yes. So long as that amulet exists, Malachai will not stop until he has brought you under his sway. And since you are the only one who can wield its power, you are probably the only one who can destroy it, as well."

I paused, carefully considering her words. *Destroy the amulet?* Yes. It was the only way to stop Malachai.

"The Tidecaller's Amulet must be destroyed," I agreed. "But I don't have a ship, and no captain will sign me. Alone, how can I find this amulet before Malachai?"

"You're not alone, Samuel," Jason assured me. "With our influence at court, we'll help you secure a royal commission. That should give you the resources you'll need."

"A royal commission?" I asked. "Are you sure you can get that?"

Julietta nodded. "I'm sure that King Leander will grant us an audience. And with Jason and me to vouch for you, I have no doubt you'll receive the full backing of the crown."

I let out a deep breath. To go from a shaggy-haired outcast unable to find a ship, to a man with a royal commission granting his pick of the fleet? It seemed like more than I could hope for. Nevertheless, Jason and Julietta seemed confident.

"Thank you," I said, swallowing my doubts.

Jason put a hand on my shoulder. "We're here for you, Samuel. My seafaring days may be over, but we'll do everything in our power to help you."

"Indeed," said Julietta, affirming his words. "We'll present your case to the king tomorrow at court. You'll have your commission by dusk."

A spark of hope ignited within me. If Julietta was right, this would change everything. It was only a start, of course. Whether or not it came to anything would be up to me. But I was ready. Wherever the amulet might be hidden, it had to be destroyed.

In Which I Receive a Royal Commission and Sign On With a Merry Crew

Lady Julietta glided over the polished stone floors of Castle Caravelia with effortless grace. Her steps echoed off the marble columns as she led me toward the throne at the head of the chamber. Dressed as she was in a flowing gown of deep blue velvet, I couldn't help but feel like a scrappy stray beside a well-groomed pedigree.

"Relax, Samuel," she said quietly. "You're not a servant here."

"Thanks," I muttered back.

She smiled and offered me her arm, which I took rather stiffly. A reassuring pat soothed me somewhat, and I stood just a little taller as I escorted her through the court.

"Remember, Samuel," Julietta whispered, leaning in close, "the kingdom needs your service in this hour, even if some do not acknowledge it."

"Thank you, milady," I said, trying not to be dismayed by the opulent courtiers all around us. The heady scent of their perfume made me stifle a sneeze, and I could feel the weight of their stares lingering on my common clothes and shaggy locks.

"Lady Julietta Callidor!" the herald announced.

We approached the throne, which gleamed like the morning tide under the golden rays of dawn. King Leander looked absolutely regal, with his white fur-trimmed robe, jet-black beard, and golden crown. I shifted nervously, trying very hard not to scuff the polished floor. Julietta gave a low curtsy, and I gave my deepest bow.

"Your Majesty," her voice rang through the great hall, "may I present to you Master Samuel Cox. He comes bearing word of the Tidecaller's Amulet, an ancient and arcane artifact."

All heads turned to face me. King Leander leaned forward with interest, piercing me with his gaze.

"Speak, young man," he commanded. "What is this artifact?"

Julietta touched my arm. I took a deep breath.

"Your Majesty, the Tidecaller's Amulet is an ancient magical artifact that holds the power to command the tides. Until now, it has been lost to history, but there are those among us who seek to recover it, I suspect for evil purposes."

King Leander frowned. "Evil purposes, you say?"

"Yes, Your Majesty. They are part of an underground cult, led by a dark sorcerer named Malachai. Just last night, I escaped being kidnapped by them."

A rumble of hushed conversations arose among the courtiers. They seemed genuinely shocked to hear of a dangerous cult within their midst, though my scalp tingled as my magic sensed some hidden members of the cult among them. All the more reason to get out of there quickly.

King Leander clenched his fists. "A cult of dark magic within my kingdom? We must uproot it at once!"

"I agree, Your Majesty. For that reason, I believe it is my duty to find and destroy this amulet before it falls into the wrong hands."

He eyed me skeptically. "And what makes you uniquely suited to this task?"

A murmur of doubt arose from the court, but before I could falter, Julietta stepped forward.

"Master Cox is indeed uniquely capable, Your Majesty. In fact, he is the only one who can wield the power of the amulet, let alone destroy it."

"Is that so?" King Leander mused as he stroked his beard. I nervously ran a hand through my unkempt locks, so out of place among these well-groomed courtiers.

"Lord Arion," King Leander called, summoning his court magician. "What can you tell us about this artifact?"

Lord Arion glided forward, his dark cloak trailing behind him as he approached the throne. His expression was grave, his eyes filled with concern.

"Your Majesty, the Tidecaller's Amulet is indeed an ancient and powerful artifact. In times of old, it has proven the downfall of many great kingdoms across the seas. However, we know little of it except that it has been lost."

"Can its powers be used for good?" Leander asked.

Lord Arion drew a sharp breath, his long beard trembling. "Of course, Your Majesty, but in this mortal realm, evil tends to overshadow good where matters of power are concerned. In my estimation, Master Cox's counsel about destroying the amulet is quite sound."

King Leander nodded thoughtfully. "And are there any others besides this young man who can destroy it?"

"I would have to search the tomes to be sure. And know his pedigree. The lore is unclear on this matter."

"Your Majesty, if I may," Julietta gently interjected. "I have known Master Cox for some time and can vouch for him. He sailed with my husband, Sir Jason, for many years. I know of his loyalty to the crown, and I am confident that he has the skills and determination to succeed."

"His appearance is... unorthodox, for a champion of the realm," one of the courtiers murmured loudly. Julietta locked onto him with her steely-eyed gaze.

"Do not be deceived by appearances. Samuel possesses a powerful gift of magic, which flows to him through his hair. Should he ever cut it, that gift would be lost."

"Is that why only he can wield the power of the amulet?" King Leander asked.

I bowed deeply. "Possibly, Your Majesty, but I do not know for sure. In fact, there is much that I still do not know."

"Then how do you know what you do?"

I swallowed, looking to Julietta for guidance. She smiled, silently urging me to speak the truth.

"The amulet was shown to me in a vision I received while I was held captive by Malachai and his followers. It's... difficult to describe, Your Majesty but while I was in that vision, I both saw and felt its power."

"The cultists certainly believe he is the key," Julietta pointed out. "Otherwise, they would not have gone to the trouble of kidnapping him."

"And how do we know that he is not still under their sway, even now?" the king asked.

"Your Majesty," said Julietta, curtsying once again. "Last night, Master Cox fled to our estate, seeking refuge. When questioned, he told us everything he knew. We have no reason to believe that he has lied to us. Indeed, we have every reason to believe that he has told us the truth."

King Leander sat back on his ornate throne, stroking his beard in thought. I bit my lip, awaiting his response.

"Very well," he said at length. "Master Cox, I shall grant you a royal commission to find and destroy this cursed artifact. May the waves and winds favor your journey."

Relief and gratitude surged within me. "Thank you, Your Majesty," I said, bowing low.

The court scribe swiftly wrote up the commission on a sheet of parchment, and King Leander pressed his own seal into the wax. My heart leaped as I graciously accepted it from the king's hand.

"Go with my blessing. And return with victory."

Julietta guided me swiftly into the hallway, her long gown swishing softly along the polished floor. "You did well there," she said, her green eyes glinting.

I nodded. "Thank you for speaking on my behalf."

"Think nothing of it. I know you will succeed."

We walked in comfortable silence through the halls of the castle, out to the central courtyard. Despite how she downplayed her own efforts, I knew that Julietta had put her reputation on the line for me. For that, I felt deeply grateful.

"What are your plans now, Samuel?" she asked. "Now that you have your commission, to whom will you go?"

It was a fair question. With the king's parchment in my hand, I had my pick of any ship in the harbor. Upon our successful return, the royal treasury would compensate us accordingly.

"Not the King's Fleet," I heard myself say, suddenly remembering the feeling of hidden cultists among the nobility. "The cult may have already infiltrated their ranks."

"Then whom?" she asked, giving me a worried look.

"A privateer crew, I think. They live by their wits, and their ships are faster than most. Besides, they have a lot more freedom on the open seas."

Julietta pursed her lips in thought. "I think I know a privateer captain who may be just the person you're looking for. She's unconventional, but she's one of the best sailors I've ever met."

I raised an eyebrow. "Who is that?"

"Captain Leona Black."

"Ah," I said, brightening at her name. "Is Captain Black in port right now?"

"Indeed. With her letter of marque and your royal commission, she'll be sure to take you on."

Captain Leona Black, I mused. We'd only worked together once, on the voyage that had ended in my friend Jason's knighthood, but I knew her for a competent and formidable captain. She had a bit of a flamboyant streak, like most privateers, but that was no impediment. The only reason I hadn't looked to her for work was that she already had a ship's mage.

"I will go to her immediately."

"Good," she said. "And until we meet again, may the winds always favor you."

I grinned. "A sea mage casts his own wind."

"Even so," she answered, returning my wry smile. "Take care of yourself, Samuel, and return with victory."

The *Ebony Eagle* was a small but sleek vessel, her hull painted black with gold trim. Her prow was long and narrow, and her bowsprit jutted out like a narwhal's tusk. From the looks of it, her sails had been recently replaced. Though they were furled like the wings of a resting gull, I had no doubt they would look magnificent when she took to sea.

Leona Black stared down at me from the *Eagle*'s aftcastle as I approached. She wore knee-high boots and tight leather breeches, with a frilly white shirt and a brightly colored jerkin. Her long black hair was pulled back in a tight, snake-like braid, and her piercing green eyes glinted like emeralds.

"Samuel Cox," she said, recognizing me at once. "It's been a while."

"You remember me, Captain Black?"

She scoffed and folded her arms. "I wouldn't soon forget Jason's shaggy-haired mage."

My heart fell, but before I could open my mouth to speak, she laughed.

"Well, don't just stand there like a fool. Come and tell me what brings a mongrel like you to my ship. Not begging for scraps, I hope."

I hesitated only a moment before crossing the gangplank and stepping onto the deck. Leona came down and offered a warm handshake that somewhat alleviated my concerns. She and Jason had been rivals for a time, but they had never been unfriendly.

"Not at all," I said, withdrawing the sheet of parchment I'd received from the king. "I'm here because of this."

"Eh?"

"It's a royal commission," I explained, handing it to her. "The king wants me to find and destroy a dangerous magical artifact, known as the Tidecaller's Amulet. I can think of no one better suited for such a mission than you, Captain Black."

Leona threw back her head and let out a hearty laugh. "Flattery will get you everywhere, my friend. But come, let's discuss this over a pint. And please—call me Leona."

I wasn't sure what to expect as I followed her into the cabin. The musky aroma of aged wood mingled with the salty sea breeze as she led me through a sturdy door into her quarters. Sunlight streamed through the porthole windows, casting a golden glow over her luxurious but well-worn furniture. Dazzling treasures adorned the walls, while a richly woven rug covered the planks of the floor. How much of this had she plundered in her many long voyages beyond Caravelia's home waters? Likely all of it.

In the center of the room stood a large wooden desk, cluttered with parchment papers, a golden compass, and other navigation tools. Leona sat on a tall leather-cushioned stool, motioning for me to sit across from her.

"Explain this dangerous artifact," she demanded.

I hesitated, suddenly self-conscious of how insane my explanation would surely sound. But from the way she curiously leaned forward, I knew my best course was to tell her everything.

"This artifact, the Tidecaller's Amulet, grants its wearer control over the tides. It has the power to cause destruction on a massive scale. I am the only one who can wield its power."

"You?"

"Yes." I took a deep breath, doing my best to return her gaze. "There's also an underground cult seeking the amulet, led by a dark sorcerer named Malachai. They've already tried to turn me to their cause, to wield the amulet's power in pursuit of their evil purposes."

Leona nodded and reached out for the commission, taking a few moments to read it. "This sounds like a tale fit for the bards," she said, raising an eyebrow. "And you say this cult is after you?"

"Aye. If they kidnap me again, they'll stop at nothing to break me. We have to find the amulet and destroy it, before it—or I—fall into their hands.

"And what makes you think I would want to get involved?"

"Because you have so much experience with this kind of mission," I said, recalling our past adventures. "Besides, with your letter of marque from the king, you have more freedom than most."

"What exactly is your plan?"

I told her about the vision that Malachai had given me, and the island I'd seen at the end of it. She rolled out several maps, which we examined carefully, but it wasn't until the fourth or fifth one that I sensed a glimmer of recognition.

"There," I said, pointing. "That's the island I saw."

"The Cerulean Sea," Leona muttered. "It's a long voyage, but well within our capabilities. Especially with a mage like you filling our sails."

My heart leaped. "You'll sign me on then?"

"Sign you on? My lad, with a royal commission like that, I'll be the one working for you—though on the high seas, distinctions like that matter little."

"Of course," I said, feeling relief wash over me. "But what about your mage?"

"Merida? She retired not long ago. Felt it was time for a new chapter. Took her shares and left the seafaring life behind."

"Truly?" I said. "I couldn't imagine giving it up."

Leona chuckled. "That's the trouble with privateering, Sam. As soon as you find success, half your crew's liable to leave."

"Well, then, I suppose I'm at your disposal, Captain," I said with a grin.

"We'll have to leave immediately, of course, to evade that pesky cult," Leona replied with a smile of her own.

"Under cover of darkness, then?"

"Good idea. We've already taken on water and supplies, so we can leave at a moment's notice. The hunt for that tide-calling trinket begins now."

I let out a sigh of relief as Leona handed me a glass filled with rum. Together, we raised our glasses in a toast.

"To the voyage," I said.

"Aye. May it find its end with us."

I drank deeply from my glass, feeling it strengthen my resolve. "To the end," I echoed.

The docks were eerily quiet as the crew of the *Ebony Eagle* made ready to sail. Above me, the stars slowly faded before the first hints of dawn. It was rare for ships to leave the harbor this early, when there wasn't much light to sail by. Which made it the perfect time for us to slip out.

"Ready?" Leona asked, her hands firmly gripping the helm. Her cat-like figure was silhouetted against the distant torchlight of the city and the growing purple glow behind the mountains to our east.

"Aye," I told her, running a hand through my hair. "Give the word, and I'll fill our sails."

"Softly," she urged with a glance back at the shore. Then, in hushed tones, she signaled the crew to hoist the anchor and unfurl the sails. I watched as they carried out her orders, their movements fluid and precise.

I summoned a slight breeze, and the ship pulled away from the dock. The waters were calm, and the

Ebony Eagle glided softly forward, barely leaving any wake. In spite of the tension in the air, my heart leaped as the harbor slowly receded behind us.

"It's been too long," I whispered to myself.

"Eh?" said Leona.

"I was just telling myself that it's been too long since I was on the water."

She nodded, a smirk playing on her lips. "Remember that, when the days are long and the seas are rough."

"I will," I promised.

The gulls' cries faded as we left the harbor and rounded the cape at the mouth of the bay in the dark, beneath the Adamantine Colossus. The sails billowed as I raised my hands to fill them, and with a heave, the *Ebony Eagle* turned and broke for the open sea.

"We'll bear south once we're out of sight of land," Leona said, her dark hair whipping in the salty breeze. "If your visions are anything to go by, that's where we'll find the amulet."

I nodded. The ship lurched a little, and I gripped the railing for support. We were fully committed now. The horizon stretched out before us, marked only by the shimmering reflection of the sky.

As dawn slowly lightened the sky behind us, a tiny speck appeared on the edge of that narrow line. A sense of unease slowly grew in my stomach as I realized it was growing larger, approaching us.

"Leona, what is that?"

She narrowed her eyes, her body suddenly tense. "I don't know, Sam. Climb up to the crow's nest and see if you can't get a better view."

The ratlines creaked beneath my feet as I ascended the rigging to the top of the mast. From the crow's nest, I squinted against the wind at the horizon, casting a spell to enhance my vision. Whoever was on that ship, they were gaining on us, their sails billowing in the wind.

"Leona!" I shouted. "Red sails! And they're definitely following us!"

"Hard to port!" she bellowed, urging her crew to action as she deftly turned the wheel. "We'll lose those yellow-bellies in the morning fog."

But the mists were not as thick as she thought. There was no way I could not keep up my windcasting without totally dispelling them. From my vantage point, I could see that the ship after us was coming closer. My heart began to pound a little, and I felt a familiar surge of magic grow within me. It demanded release almost with a mind of its own, itching to show its might against our pursuers.

"It's no use," I shouted. "They're still following us."

"Then we'll turn and fight," Leona said grimly. "Get down here, Sam."

Quickly, I scurried down the rigging and joined her atop the aftcastle, preparing myself for battle. My heart raced from exhilaration and fear.

"Ahoy!" Leona shouted as the outline of the ship became clear through the midst of the fog. "Identify yourself!"

There was a long, pregnant pause as we waited for the other ship to respond. Our archers drew their arrows, and I lifted my hands, preparing to cast the first spell.

"Captain Soren White of His Majesty's Ship, the *Black Sword,"* came the answer. "We're here to escort the *Ebony Eagle."*

Leona frowned. "Escort? Since when do Fleet officers take such an interest in a privateer's course?"

And how do we know they are who they say they are? I thought but did not say.

Then the ship pulled alongside us, and I saw who stood at the helm. My stomach fell, even as relief surged through me. It was none other than Soren, my old nemesis from my days in the King's Fleet.

"Since your voyage has been commissioned from the king," he answered back.

Leona swore under her breath before turning to her men. "Stand down," she ordered. "These are friends, not foes."

"'Friend' might be too strong a word," I muttered.

Even after all these years, my feud with Soren still rankled. We had both served the king the best we could, but where I had struggled, he had flourished. Where I had garnered rebukes, he had garnered praise. In a moment of frustration, our personalities had clashed, and he'd used that as a pretext to turn everyone in the fleet against me. He was largely the reason that I'd dropped out and signed on with Jason so long ago.

"Well, well, well!" Soren called out from across the waters. "If it isn't shaggy-haired Samuel himself."

"Hello, Soren," I answered.

"You picked a strange ship for your mission," he shouted with a wry grin. "Though given your history, I can see why you wouldn't come to the King's Fleet."

Leona bristled. "Whose ship are you calling 'strange'?"

"I mean no offense, Captain Black. But now that we are here to escort you, we'll see that no sorcery stands in your way."

Leona swore loudly. "We can handle ourselves."

"Of course you can. And with us, you can handle even more." He gave me a pointed look. "Do try to keep up, Samuel. There's no dropping out this time."

I clenched my fists, but before I could think of a retort, Soren's ship had already pulled out of earshot. Leona swore again and shook her head.

"How in the hell did that pompous fool find out that we'd left?"

I sighed. "When he heard that I'd gone to you with the commission, he probably guessed we'd try to ship out before dawn. Any chance we can shake him?"

She shook her head. "The *Eagle* is fast enough to lose them, but we don't want to arouse any suspicions. Best to just avoid them as much as we can."

I had been afraid she would say something like that. And as the sun peeked over the foggy horizon to our east, making the mists sparkle magnificently, the pleasure of the sight was tempered by the knowledge that Soren would never be far away.

In Which We Encounter Setbacks and a Rivalry That Nearly Comes to Blows

Our voyage to the Cerulean Sea was long and tedious, punctuated with moments of sheer terror. At one point, a rogue wave nearly capsized our ship, but I detected it in time to save us from disaster. We kept a close watch the next few days, suspecting sorcery, but in the end, we decided that it must have been a natural phenomenon. The seas are full of countless perils, only a fraction of which are supernatural.

Even so, we sailed past the Cape of Desolation without much trouble. The skies were clear and the seas were placid. Which makes for a rather boring story, so I'll forbear giving you a detailed account, though Leona's sharp wit and entertaining stories relieved us a great deal from the daily monotony.

After many days, we sighted the deserted jungle island I'd identified from my vision. I recognized it at once. It appeared quite small on the horizon, but as we drew closer, it soon loomed over us, its dark green canopy teeming with life and danger.

"This is it," I murmured, squinting against the blinding light of the noonday sun. "With luck, we'll find and destroy that amulet before sundown."

Leona grinned. "You know it's never that easy."

"Aye. But we still can hope for the best."

Leona placed a hand on my shoulder. "What do you think of this place?" she asked.

I peered at the mysterious island, taking it in. It was unlike any I had ever seen. Enormous trees towered over what looked like stone structures—ruins from a fallen civilization, perhaps the one that had forged the Tidecaller's Amulet itself. It had an otherworldly feel, beautiful and foreboding. "It's breathtaking."

"Aye."

We sailed around the island twice before dropping anchor in a secluded cove. There was no sign of current habitation, though the ruins were visible from the sea. Half of Leona's crew stayed with the *Eagle*, while the rest disembarked on the launch, including Leona and myself. The crew fanned out across the beach, quickly securing it. But the search for the amulet fell to me.

"Well, Sam," she said, striding over. "Where to now?"

I grasped the scrystone compass in my hand, but it might as well have been an old, weather-worn rock for all the help it gave me. Still, I thought I sensed something up ahead.

"This way," I said, striding toward the tree line.

We followed a path into the heart of the jungle, and probably the ruins as well. Leona's men marveled at the exotic flora and fauna that surrounded us. Monkeys hooted and swung from the trees, while colorful birds flitted through the air above us. Massive ferns covered the underbrush like flags of emerald green, while vines and creepers ran up the massive trunks.

"By the gods, what is that?" one of the men exclaimed, pointing to a large basilisk lizard that splayed its neck frills in warning.

"Careful now," I cautioned. "Don't look it in the eye."

Leona chuckled softly. "You've read too many storybooks, Samuel. Still, best not to test the old wives' tales."

The jungle suddenly parted, and we found ourselves in the midst of the ruins, draped in vines and frozen in time. The amulet had to be here, somewhere amidst these silent sentinels.

"These ruins must be ancient!" one of the crew marveled.

"Stow it, you sea dogs," Leona ordered. "We're here for one thing, and Sam alone knows where it is. Stay close, and keep your eyes peeled."

My heart pounded as I tried to recall the vision. But when I sent out my magic, probing for the amulet, it came back to me empty. I hardly knew where to start.

"Well, Sam," Leona muttered. "Have anything for us?"

I closed my eyes and used my abilities again, this time sensing for any trace of magic. When I opened my eyes again, I could see faint glimmers on the edge of my vision.

"This way," I told her, motioning toward the greatest cluster of lingering light.

We searched the ruins for hours, moving carefully over the piles of rubble and entangling roots. Our wonder quickly turned to disappointment and frustration, as all we uncovered was some worthless shards of pottery and mostly decayed bones.

"Are we sure this is the right place?" one of the crew asked me quietly, out of Leona's earshot.

"It has to be," I replied, though I was starting to lose confidence. What I'd first taken for a magical impression now seemed to be nothing but wishful thinking.

"Found something!" someone cried from the next courtyard over. But it was merely a broken pedestal with a fallen statue.

Frustration began to rise like bile in my chest. On the other side of the courtyard, Leona tapped her foot impatiently as she scanned the ruins with her sharp, searching eyes.

"Found anything?" I asked.

"Nothing but death and decay," she replied, kicking a small stone. "This place is naught but an empty grave."

I clenched my jaw and forced myself to keep moving, ignoring the growing sense of unease in my gut. The sun already hung low in the afternoon sky. At best, we had only a few hours of daylight left. If Malachai's minions had somehow traced us here, they could set up an ambush and catch us unawares. Better to conclude our search and be gone before dark.

We pressed further into the ruins, the shadows growing ever longer as we did. Suddenly, I stumbled upon a hidden chamber, its walls adorned with ancient runes.

"Leona!"

Her footsteps sounded behind me, leather boots crunching the foliage underfoot. "What is it, Sam?"

"I think this may be it. Here—help me."

With our bare hands, we dug out the ground immediately in front of the chamber's buried entrance. Some nearby members of the crew quickly joined us, and soon, we had it excavated. I pressed my hand to the stone, and it gave way under my touch, parting with a deafening groan.

I cast a spell of illumination and sent an orb of glowing light inside. The ruins here looked to be in better condition than the rest of what we'd seen. Not sensing any no obvious dangers, I took a step inside.

"Wait here," I said, motioning for the others to stay behind me. I crouched a little and peered down the narrow hall. Was that an altar in the next room? There was an indentation on it that was just the right size for an artifact like the amulet.

I rushed forward, hardly daring to breathe. I suddenly had the distinct impression that this was the resting place of the amulet that I had seen in my vision. But my heart sank as I saw that the altar was empty. The amulet was gone.

"What is it?" asked Leona, ignoring my directions as she rushed to my side.

"It's gone," I told her. "This is where the amulet should be, but..."

Leona swore. "You think we should keep looking?"

"What's the point?" I asked, shaking my head. "Whoever took the amulet wouldn't have hidden it anywhere else on the island. Wherever it is, it's gone."

She thought about that for a long moment, scratching her chin. Finally, she grunted.

"Let's get back to the ship and figure out our next move."

"Aye," I said reluctantly, feeling defeated and lost. But what else could we do? The scrystone compass was worse than useless, and every time I sent my magic out, it returned to me as empty as this forgotten altar. Wherever the amulet had been, it wasn't here anymore.

The hot afternoon sun sat low in the sky as we trudged back to the beach. In the face of our disappointment, the tropical heat felt oppressive, the jungle air thick and unbearably humid. I loosened the collar of my sweat-stained shirt, eager to feel the firmness of the *Ebony Eagle's* deck beneath my feet instead of shifting sand.

But as we caught sight of the breakers, we saw that we were not alone. A second ship had anchored in the cove, and a launch was coming ashore only a few hundred yards from where we'd beached ours. As we watched, the rowers pulled up their oars, and several men jumped into the shallow water to pull it ashore.

"Who's that?" I asked, frowning.

Leona scowled. "Isadora Stone."

I narrowed my eyes. "Isadora who?"

It was then that I saw their captain, a woman not unlike Leona herself, except that her hair was flaxen instead of midnight black. She wore a double-peaked hat with a peacock's plume, her long blond hair pulled back into a thick braid that reached all the way to her waist. Her features were sharp, her skin deeply tanned. She was dressed in a frilly white shirt and sleek leather jerkin, with colorful breeches and well-worn leather boots that reached almost to her knees.

"Steady, men," Leona said sulkily, her hand on the hilt of her sword. "Let's see what the sea witch wants with us." They spread out all around her, tense and ready for action.

"Who is she?" I asked. "A fellow privateer?"

"Aye. Stay close, Sam. This could get ugly."

Isadora's men pulled the launch onto the beach and protectively surrounded her as she strode toward us across the beach. "Leona," she called out, her voice warm and honeyed. "Fancy meeting you in a place like this."

"Isadora," Leona spat, as if the very name left a bad taste in her mouth. "What brings you to this charming little island in the butt-end of nowhere?"

"Same thing as you, I imagine. A certain magical amulet, perhaps?"

The fury of Leona's glare rose about a hundred degrees. "Let's make one thing clear," she said, her voice dangerously low. "You stay out of our way, and we'll stay out of yours."

The sound of swords sliding out of their sheaths alerted me at once to the danger at hand. Before our little spat could turn into a bloodbath, I rushed to place myself between the two captains.

"Let's not be hasty," I said, keeping my voice calm. "We've searched this whole island and haven't found any artifact here worth taking, magical or otherwise. Now—"

"You know, I missed the days when we used to be allies, my dear sister-in-arms," Isadora told Leona, ignoring me. "But your ambition corrupted you. You sold out."

"You lying hag," Leona snarled. "*You* betrayed *us*."

Isadora shrugged, exuding a cat-like air of nonchalance. "All right, Leona. I won't dwell on past mistakes, but let's not ignore the fact that *you* took a letter of marque, not *me*."

I winced as Leona drew her sword a few inches from its scabbard. The tension increased palpably, and I could tell that the men were itching to spill each other's blood across the hot sand. But like a pair of fighting cocks each sizing up their opponent, the two rival captains ignored everything around them.

"Don't play games, Isadora," Leona growled. "I'll send the Tidecaller's Amulet to the bottom of the sea before I let you have it."

Isadora's smile turned into a sly grin. "So, we seek the same treasure, after all."

"And it isn't here," I said, stepping between them once again. "In fact, we were just heading out of here. Must have gotten the wrong island."

"Get behind me, Sam," Leona said firmly, her eyes still fixed on her rival. "We're not going back to the ship."

I frowned. "Leona, surely you can see that there's no sense in—"

"We have *not* finished the search for the amulet. In fact, we were only getting started. Only one of us is coming away with this treasure, and I'll be damned if it's this sea witch."

Isadora threw back her head and laughed. "Sea witch? Oh, you were always one for drama."

"Watch your tongue," Leona snapped.

"Or what?"

"Or you'll be sleeping with the sharks tonight."

"Like I said," Isadora said with a smirk. "Dramatic. But no matter. Since we're both after the same treasure, we'll just have to play things out until the best captain wins."

"Which is why you'll never get your filthy little hands on it."

"Oh, you're one to talk, darling. I *know* where your hands have been."

"Stow it, Isadora. I've no time for liars like you."

"To the jungle, men!" I shouted before the catfight could turn into a bloodbath. "We've got an island to search!"

My words roused the men on both sides to action. Like water bursting out of a broken dam, the pent-up tension drove them into a mad dash for the jungle, away from their two feuding captains. I sighed in relief.

"Time to go," I said, putting a hand on Leona's shoulder.

"This isn't the last you've seen of me, Stone!" she shouted venomously. "And the next time we meet, we'll settle this score!"

"After I beat you to the prize, you mean?"

It took all of my strength to keep Leona from charging past me, no doubt to bury her blade in her opponent's breast. But I held firm.

"Let me go!" Leona fumed as I pushed her back out of earshot. "I can't let that sea witch have the last word—I *can't*!"

"Just let it go, Leona," I said in my most soothing voice.

"But—"

"I said, let it go!"

She pouted a little, then shoved me away as she stalked off into the jungle with what little dignity she had left. I followed close behind her, partly to keep her from running back, and partly to help her see reason.

"Now that her men are spreading out, let's gather everyone back to the beach and give her the slip. After all—"

"No. We don't leave this island until she does."

I frowned. "What do you mean? We already know that the amulet isn't here."

"Do we?" she asked.

"Uh—"

Without another word, she stormed toward the jungle, following her men. The awful sinking feeling in my gut returned as I realized that Leona wasn't about to leave. We could look under every stone in the ruins twice over, but so long as Isadora was still here, Leona wouldn't take the chance that we'd somehow missed something.

"Keep moving," Leona yelled back at me over her shoulder.

The sun, which before had been sweltering, now seemed ready to melt me into a puddle. And as I plunged into the thick, muggy jungle on what was surely a fool's errand, all I could wonder was whether Leona's pride would break before the cultists caught up to us.

We pushed through the jungle until we came back to the ruins. The crumbling structures seemed a lot less awe-inspiring the second time.

"Stay alert," Leona growled. "We can't let Isadora win."

That might be true, but what was the point of staying here when the amulet was almost certainly somewhere else? If I couldn't find it, I doubted that Isadora could. But as much as I wanted to protest, Leona's eyes blazed with such fury that I knew it would be a mistake to do so. Instead, all I could do was try to keep up as I swatted at the insects buzzing around my head and wiped the sweat from my face.

"There," said Leona, pointing to a cluster of outlying structures. "We haven't tried there yet."

"I don't know," I said, reaching out with my magic. It came back to me empty, and I shook my head. "I really don't think that the amulet—"

"Stow it, Sam." She turned to the rest of the crew. "Fan out, men, but don't stray too far."

With a sigh, I pushed ahead, knowing that this was, at best, a supreme waste of our time. But as I followed the rest of the crew under the crumbling archway, I suddenly sensed danger as well.

I called out in alarm, but it was too late. A sinkhole opened beneath the man at the front, and he fell into it with a blood-curdling scream.

Without thinking, I leaped in after him, using my magic to soften our fall. The darkness swallowed us, and we rolled and tumbled together, abruptly coming to rest at the muddy bottom.

"Watch out, Sam!" Leona called after me—as if her words were any help now. I groaned and stood unsteadily on my feet, checking myself for broken bones.

At that moment, a snake slithered across my feet. I jumped, nearly stepping on another, which hissed and reared. The entire hole was filled with them, some sort of nest.

Leona's crewman sliced the beast in half with a yell, but that only seemed to enrage the others, who slithered so much that it soon seemed the floor itself was writhing.

"Stand back," I said. Then, using my magic, I cast a fire spell on the ground immediately around us. The snakes pulled back, hissing and spitting with rage as the acrid smell of singed meat met our noses.

"Ha!" Leona's crewman said. "That'll show 'em!"

"We have to get out of here," I said, looking up. But the walls of the hole were far too muddy and steep for us to climb.

"Hang on, Sam!" Leona shouted. A few moments later, she threw down a rope—and just in time. Normally, fire would have driven the snakes away, but with nowhere to flee, they were quickly becoming emboldened, burning as they tried to strike us through the flames. I couldn't keep up the spell forever, and it would only take one good bite to kill either of us.

I helped Leona's crewman climb up first. He scrambled up the rope as if it were rigging on a ship, quickly reaching the top. I was much slower, but with the help of the others, I was soon up and out, panting on the ground.

"Good thinking, Sam," said Leona. "That was too close."

"There's nothing on this island," I snapped at her, unable to hold myself back. "We're wasting our time and risking the lives of your men. We should leave this place to Isadora—she can have it, for all I care."

My appeal to the welfare of her men finally reached her. She was not the sort of leader to throw their lives away.

"All right," Leona said reluctantly. "We'll confront her directly. No sense in dragging this out."

We found the other privateer crew in the midst of the ruins we'd already searched, poring carefully over the crumbling stone structures. Isadora stood near her ship's sea mage, an enormous brown-skinned islander with tattoos covering every inch of his skin. The ink under his skin glowed as he cast his spells, and my hair tingled at the sight of him. I kept a respectful distance.

Leona, on the other hand, walked right up to Isadora without a care.

"This island isn't big enough for the two of us," she said angrily, forgetting about leaving this place behind. Isadora's very presence was a challenge, and that was all that mattered to her now.

Isadora regarded her coolly, her men quickly flocking to her. Leona's men advanced as well, quietly drawing their swords.

"Go back to your ship, Leona. Or shall I have my men send you there?"

Inwardly, I groaned. There was little chance now that Leona would back down without a bloody fight.

"Enough of your games, you sea witch," Leona snapped. "Where's the amulet?"

"We don't have it."

"The hell you don't! My sea mage saw it here, on this island. If you didn't take it, who did?"

Isadora smirked. "Wouldn't you like to know?"

Leona scowled, her hand on the hilt of her sword. "Speak plainly or—"

"To Captain Black!" a voice bellowed from the underbrush—and without warning, a troop of Caravelian soldiers burst through the thick foliage. Isadora's crew, caught unawares, pulled back on either side, allowing the soldiers to come between us. Soren stood at their head, his sword drawn.

"Stand down," he said, eyeing Leona and Isadora coolly. "This island is now under the protection of King Leander's fleet."

Outnumbered and outflanked, Isadora had little choice but to retreat. Her smirk turned to an ugly scowl, and she waved to her men, who fell back into the jungle.

"This isn't the last you've seen of me, Black," she shouted over her shoulder.

"Ha!" Leona laughed. "Run, you yellow-bellied traitor! Run like the coward you are!"

"Soren," I said, acknowledging my old nemesis with an uneasy nod.

Soren sighed as he sheathed his sword. "In the future, do try to stay out of trouble, Samuel. I won't always be there to bail you out."

The hair on my neck bristled. "We were doing just fine, until—"

"Yes, yes, of course." He turned to Leona and saluted. "At your service, Captain Black."

"Impeccable timing," she muttered reluctantly. "But why didn't you stop that sea witch before she landed?"

He raised an eyebrow. "I thought she was a friend of yours. You do have a history, do you not?"

"Yeah," said Leona, spitting on the ground. "You could say that."

"We can handle our own affairs, Soren," I told him. "This is our commission, not yours."

"And you're doing quite a splendid job of screwing it up," he said, eyeing me coolly. "It still seems to be what you're best at."

"Sam is right, Soren," Leona told him. "Thanks for your help, but you can stay out of our way from now on."

The king's officer bowed with a flourish. "Captain Black, I wouldn't presume to obstruct your mission in any way. But the next time you need us, I promise, we'll be there."

Leona folded her arms. As much as she wanted to send him back to Caravelia, we both knew that

Soren's intervention was the only thing that had prevented a bloody battle. So we watched in silence as he marched his men back through the jungle toward the beach, leaving us alone.

"What now?" I asked after he was gone.

"Let's get off this damned rock," Leona muttered. "Move out, men. To the *Eagle*."

I nodded, relieved to see that she'd finally seen reason. Still, as we trudged down the path toward the sound of the distant breakers, I couldn't help but feel a tinge of disappointment that we were returning empty-handed.

In Which We Find a Fragment, and My Hair Nearly Seals My Doom

The vast Cerulean Sea spread out before us, its deep blue waters sparkling under the light of the tropical sun. I tightened my grip on the railing of the *Ebony Eagle,* knowing that somewhere across that vast expanse, the Tidecaller's Amulet was waiting to be found. But where?

Unlike the Azure Sea, the Cerulean Sea was dotted with hundreds of islands, most of them small and uninhabited. The few people who made their homes in these sweltering latitudes were barely civilized enough to trade with, and the ocean itself was nearly three times the size of the Azure Sea. We could spend a whole lifetime exploring these savage waters and never see a tenth of it.

As I brooded over these thoughts, blinking through the salty mist, I suddenly felt a premonition that made my very bones quake. The last time I'd felt something similar had been when I'd first had the vision of the amulet in Caravelia. Was it near, then? My heart leaped at the thought. I reached a trembling hand for the compass hanging around my neck and found that the needle was spinning.

"Leona," I yelled, hurrying back to the aftcastle. Leona peered down at me, her green eyes ablaze.

"What is it, Sam?"

"I can feel the Tidecaller's Amulet! It must be close!"

Leona frowned. "But the nearest land is ten leagues away."

"Then it must be below us, in the water."

She pondered this for a moment as I eagerly climbed the steps to join her on the upper deck. She had every right to be skeptical. In all directions, the open ocean surrounded us, with none of the chattering shorebirds we would find nearer land. And yet, I could not deny what I had felt.

"At the bottom of the sea?" she said skeptically. "How sure are you, Sam?"

"Absolutely certain."

She sighed. "The last time we followed your feelings, we wound up chasing ghosts. It's no small thing to drop anchor this far from land."

"Just give me an hour," I begged. "Please. The amulet's down there—I can feel it in my bones."

Leona gazed out across the horizon as if deep in thought. But after a long moment, she nodded grimly and began barking orders to her crew.

"Lower the sails," she commanded firmly. "Walk back the anchor."

"Aye!" her men shouted as they hurried to carry out her commands.

She turned back to face me, her expression grim. "I guess we'll see if water sea is shallow enough to anchor. But there's a storm brewing on the horizon, Sam. We can't afford to linger, Sam."

"I understand."

I waited gratefully as the crew carried out her orders. They tossed the anchor into the sea, waiting as the line ran out. For a time, it looked like we might run out of rope before it reached the bottom, but the line went slack just before the end.

"That's more than a hundred fathoms," Leona muttered. "Are you still sure about this, Sam?"

"More than ever," I said, casting off my shirt and boots. "My magic will sustain me while I'm down there."

"Be quick. If the wind turns, it'll bring that storm right down..." She paused and held up her hand. "Wait here. I'll be back."

I frowned as I waited impatiently for her to return. The sun was hot and the breeze was comfortably warm, but at a hundred fathoms, the water was sure to be cold. As I waited, I began casting the spells that would support me in the watery depths.

Leona returned, carrying a small, smooth, cloudy-white whisperstone. "Take this with you," she said.

"Good idea," I said, slipping it into my breech pocket and buttoning it securely shut. "I assume you have the other one?"

"Yes. Keep in touch while you're down there. If that storm comes for us, we'll have to weigh anchor, whether you're back or not. Got it?"

"Got it," I told her. Without another word, I dove off the deck and plunged into the shimmering waters.

My magic pulsed from my scalp to the ends of my hair as I ventured into the murky depths. A simple but powerful swimming spell allowed me to breathe naturally, and another kept me from being crushed. As I'd expected, the waters quickly turned cool, but a tingling sensation of warmth ran from my scalp over my whole body, protecting me from the hostile depths.

Before long, the darkness became nearly impenetrable, and I had to cast yet another spell to enhance my vision. The ocean depths were not totally devoid of light, but without my magic, I wouldn't have been able to see anything. The darkness of the abyss grew as I swam ever deeper, straining my magic to the utmost.

Just when I thought I would have to turn back, the sea floor came into view.

I marveled at the alien world all around me. Schools of iridescent fish shimmered in the watery expanse, while crabs and spiny urchins crawled along the rocky bottom, scurrying between dark clumps of seaweed scattered across the sandy floor. Clouds of deep-water plankton enveloped me, while the distant sound of whale song told me that a pod was nearby.

With my magically enhanced eyes, I spied the broken hulk of a large ship. My heart raced at the sight as I felt the premonition again. The Tidecaller's Amulet must have sunk with the ship.

Leona's voice came inside my mind, as clearly as if she were standing beside me. "Can you hear me, Sam?"

"Aye," I said, channeling my voice through the whisperstone. "There's a sunken ship down here, and I think the amulet is inside."

"Good. Make it fast—the winds are shifting."

"Got it," I replied and kicked harder, keeping a steady pace through the eerie depths. The shipwreck grew closer, its once-majestic structure looming like the skeletal remains of a colossal beast. A few wispy tatters of sail hung from the yards, while fish darted through broken and shattered beams. I swam slowly around toward the stern, where a sigil was etched into the wood. Despite the innumerable years, the coat of arms was still faintly visible.

"I'm going inside," I whispered through the stone.

"Good luck, Sam," Leona answered.

The fragile, waterlogged timbers groaned ever so slightly as I swam through them. I made a methodical search, starting at the stern and working toward the bow, from the shattered deck to the sand-filled hold. There was all manner of treasure on the ship: gold coins, gem-studded goblets, and finely-made swords, their blades cankered but the hilts still intact. But no amulet.

"Found it?" Leona asked.

"Not yet," I told her, returning to the few waterlogged chests I'd seen in the aftcastle. "It's got to be here, though. Just give me more time."

"I've already given you about all the time we have, Sam. The storm will be here soon."

Her words hit me like a splash of cold reality. It felt like only moments had passed in this dreamlike underwater world. My movements became increasingly frantic as I searched the chaotic mess of overturned crates and broken barrels, their contents ravaged and lost long ago. Frustration began to rise within me as I sensed the amulet even closer than before, so close that it almost seemed to be taunting me. But none of my desperate efforts bore fruit.

"Stay calm," I told myself, pausing to take a breath. "This isn't going to get you anywhere."

As I let the negative energy flow out of me, I suddenly remembered the scrystone compass around my neck. Clutching it in my hand, I gazed into its depths, easing back on my vision enhancing spell to block out all else. As I did so, an image of a chest came into my mind, as clear as Leona's voice through the whisperstone. Where had I seen that chest? The captain's cabin!

My heart surged as I swam up through the creaking timbers, taking a shortcut through a breach in the hull. In a hidden niche beneath one of the floorboards, I found the chest that I'd seen in the scrystone. With trembling fingers, I drew out my knife and began to pry it open.

"Sam?" Leona's voice came, even more urgent this time.

"Still here," I muttered, grunting with effort. "The lid of this chest is stuck."

"The storm is nearly upon us, Sam. We're weighing the anchor now."

"All right. I'll be right up."

My heart pounded as I finally cracked the lid. Inside, resting on a bed of decaying velvet, was a single black stone, set within a large silver pendant. Its polished surface gleamed in the dim light. I reached for it eagerly, then frowned.

"What do you see, Sam?"

"It's here, but it's broken. One piece of four. The amulet isn't whole."

"Damnation," she swore. "Any sign of the other fragments?"

"None," I said, reaching out with my magic to make sure. "It must have been broken before they brought it aboard."

She swore again, the frustration in her voice echoing my own. "Those other pieces could be anywhere by now."

"Yes, but at least it's something. I'm coming back now."

"All right, Sam. See you topside."

I slipped the pendant chain around my neck, letting it clatter against the compass and my mother's locket. A couple of tugs reassured me that the amulet was secure. But as I swam up through the cabin doorway, a sharp pain shot across my scalp.

"Ow!"

"Sam, what's happening?"

I reached back, feeling at the nail that had caught in my hair. A sharp burst of adrenaline surged through me as I realized I was trapped.

"My hair—it's caught on something."

"Can you free yourself?"

"I'm trying, but it might take a minute."

"We don't have a minute, Sam. The storm is almost upon us."

My magic was the only thing keeping me alive. If I pulled too hard and ripped out my hair, this shipwreck would become my tomb. In just a few minutes, though, the *Ebony Eagle* would leave without me. My powers were already strained to their limit, and I didn't know how long I had before my magic gave out simply from exhaustion.

"Just cut your hair, Sam!" Leona urged.

"I can't—I'll lose my magic!"

At that moment, a shadow passed overhead, cutting through the dim light above. My heart leaped as I saw what was hunting me.

"What was that?"

"Sharks," I said, keeping my voice low so as not to attract their attention. But as I watched, nearly a dozen joined the deadly dance. It seemed that they could smell my fear as they circled ever closer.

My heart raced with terror. Was this my end? Trapped at the bottom of the unforgiving ocean, alone at the mercy of these savage creatures?

In that moment, they made their attack.

The nearest one turned and darted straight at me, opening its fearsomely toothed maw. Without thinking, I clutched the amulet in my hand. A surge of energy coursed through my body, unleashing a blinding burst of light and power. The shark swerved at the last minute, scattering with the others in every direction.

"Sam? What was that?"

"My hair," I said, suddenly realizing that I was free. The unexpected burst of magic must have jarred me loose. My heart skipped a beat, and I couldn't help but laugh for joy.

"Celebrate later," Leona snapped. "Come up, now!"

The burst of power from the amulet had all but drained me, and with what remained of my ebbing strength, I swam straight up toward the light. Even as the surface came into sight, I had to hold my breath as the swimming spell gave out. I kicked wildly, my lungs feeling as if they would burst.

Finally, I broke through the surface. In the air above me, the storm raged, dark clouds churning the waters and unleashing torrents of rain. The wind howled in my ears as I gasped for breath, the waves threatening to pull me back under.

I clutched at my neck. Thankfully, the amulet was still there.

In the distance, I caught sight of the *Ebony Eagle* fighting against the waves. With one final rush of effort, I swam as hard as I could toward her. By the time I finally reached the ship, I was almost too weak to swim any farther.

Cries sounded from the deck as they spotted me. Someone threw down a rope, and I clung to it like a lifeline as the crew hauled me up, not letting go until I'd collapsed onto the deck.

"Are you all right, Sam?" Leona asked.

"Aye," I answered, spitting up water. Then, with a grin, I held up the amulet.

She frowned and took it from me. Lightning split the sky, and the ship rocked drunkenly beneath us, but all of that seemed to fade before the sense of triumph that now filled me.

"One piece of four," she muttered, handing it back. "Any idea where to find the rest of it?"

I coughed and eased myself up to a sitting position. Around me, the crew shouted to each other as they struggled against the storm.

"Not yet," I told her. "But I'll bet we can use this one to find the rest."

"All right," she said, turning to face the wind. "First, let's get through this damned storm."

With that, she started barking orders to the crew. Lightning flashed across the darkened sky, illuminating her face. I took a deep breath and steadied myself against the railing, rallying my magic as best as I could. There was no way around it—the next few hours were going to be rough. But we'd already weathered a few storms like this one and would doubtless face many more before our journey's end.

I had no idea where our journey would take us next. Three more pieces of the amulet waited to be found. As I summoned my magic to get us through the storm, I couldn't shake the feeling that our greatest challenges were yet to come.

In Which We Befriend Some Natives and Nearly Fall Into the Wrong Hands

The sea is a fickle mistress. One moment, it can be as serene as a sleeping newborn, and the next it could scream and howl like... a not-sleeping newborn. But today, it was quiet. The waves lapped gently against the hull of our ship as we sailed into the shallow waters of the next island, looking for a place to go ashore.

"You're sure this is the place, Sam?" Leona asked beside me.

I clutched the fragment of the Tidecaller's Amulet in my hand, channeling my magic through it. Even incomplete, the power it offered me was more than I could fully understand.

"I'm not really sure of anything," I told her honestly. "But as best as I can tell, this is where the fragment is leading us. Do you want to sail around the island again, just to make sure?"

She shrugged and made a dismissive gesture. "The only certainties in life are death and robbery."

I frowned. "Isn't that supposed to be 'death and taxes'?"

"There's a difference? Personally, I prefer to deal with thieves who are honest about it. But that isn't the point. If you think this is the place, then let's head ashore and hope this relic of yours isn't leading us astray."

We dropped anchor within view of a wide, sandy beach guarded by gentle breakers. Moments later, we were rowing toward land along with a few hand-picked members of the crew.

As our launch drew closer to the island, the landscape came into sharper focus. The island rose out of the ocean dramatically, peaking at several thousand feet. A thick layer of lush vegetation cascaded down the sides of the mountain, the vibrant shades of green softening its rugged face. A pristine white beach encircled the island like a sparkling halo, completing the tranquil scene.

The *Black Sword,* Soren's ship, had finally caught up to us and was just barely visible near the horizon. Whatever dangers awaited us ashore, we would face them on our own.

As we crossed the breakers, a band of brown-skinned natives gathered on the beach. Their clothing was sparse and simple, but their flint weapons appeared to be excellently made.

"Steady," Leona urged her men, looking to me for guidance. "They're friendly, right?"

I reached out with my magic, sensing for danger, and found none. "I think so," I assured her. "At least, they don't seem to mean us harm."

"All right," said Leona, though she kept a hand on her hilt.

We rowed the rest of the way in silence, the men forming a protective ring around us as we jumped out and hauled the launch onto the sand. The natives waited for us to come to them, neither threatening nor making the first move. They stood about my height, with intricate tattoos scrawled across their beautiful dark skin. I cleared my throat nervously.

"Hello there!" I called out with a friendly wave.

"Greetings, great shaggy one," said one of their elders, a man with thick white hair. A strange sensation washed over me as I realized that I could understand his words.

"Are you all right?" Leona asked from just behind me. "What did he say?"

"He called me 'great shaggy one.'"

She frowned. "You can understand them?"

"I think so. It must be my magic."

The elder waited patiently for my response. I cleared my throat.

"We come seeking friendship and knowledge," I told him. To my astonishment, my answer was in their language.

The elder smiled. "Then come."

We followed them into the underbrush, still not sure what to expect. They seemed to be peaceful enough. Still, I kept the amulet hidden beneath my shirt, just in case.

"Your coming was foretold by our wise woman," the elder said as we walked.

"Is that so?"

"Yes. You also have the bearing and face of one of our men—though your skin is lighter than our own."

I glanced down at my arms. My skin had always seemed a bit on the swarthy side for most Caravelians, though not enough to set me apart. But now that he mentioned it, I did see some physical similarities between myself and the natives who surrounded us.

"We do not wish to stay for long," I told him. "Once we have found what we seek, we shall leave your people in peace."

"Of course, shaggy one."

We emerged from the jungle into a small village of thatched-roof huts scattered amongst the foliage. Though made of simple materials, each dwelling was excellently crafted. As the village elder (for that was what I sensed he was) led us through the community, a small crowd of women gathered curiously around us. Their clothes were woven from grass and leaves, their skin dark and weathered. Many of them wore necklaces made of seashells. Eventually, the elder guided us into a large hall at the center of the village.

"What is this place?" Leona asked, her voice low.

"Their home," I told her. "It would appear that we are their guests."

"Or their prisoners," she said, glancing around nervously.

"Don't worry. I told their elder that we don't plan to stay for very long, and he seemed to accept that."

"All right," she muttered. "Just keep your eyes open."

In the dimly lit space of the great hall, we saw the other village elders, as well as a tiny, wizened old woman who sat in a place of honor near the front.

"Welcome," she said warmly. "It has been many years since one of our own has returned to these shores."

"Thank you for having us," I replied, unsure what to make of her unusual greeting. "We come seeking knowledge, and do not wish to stay overly long."

She smiled wanly, as if at some joke that only she understood.

"How is it that I can understand you?" I asked, still confused that their language was no barrier for me. As much as I wanted to hear the story of their people, I felt that I first had to clear up that point.

"Magic speaks in many tongues," she answered cryptically. "Yours listens well. What is your name?"

"Samuel."

"Samuel," she repeated thoughtfully. "You have the bearing of one of the old ones."

"The old ones?" I asked, intrigued.

"Yes," the wise woman answered. "Our ancestors built a great civilization that once thrived in these fertile waters. They created magnificent cities, and their ships sailed far across the sea. But at the height of their glory, they seized upon the forbidden powers and brought down the wrath of the gods."

I glanced around the hall at the various totems that these people had erected. Each carving was made with obvious care. Once again, I felt something resonate deep within me, as if they spoke of memories that I had forgotten before I'd been born.

"What is she talking about?" Leona asked.

"The history of their people," I told her. "She says that their civilization once spanned all these islands, but they were destroyed by 'the wrath of the gods' at the height of their glory."

"Destroyed by natural disaster?" Leona asked softly.

"Consumed by raging waters," the wise woman confirmed—though of course, only I could understand her. I turned to face her again.

"And magic involved in this downfall?"

Her nod was slow, heavy with ancient grief. "Magic... and greed."

I wasn't sure what to say to that, so I waited patiently for her to continue. She coughed a little, then gave me a sad smile.

"You have questions," she said, gesturing for me to speak. "Please, my son. Ask what you will."

I hesitated, unsure how to proceed. But her eyes were not unkind, and these people obviously meant us no harm, so I decided on a direct approach.

"We seek an ancient artifact, known as the Tidecaller's Amulet," I said, pulling out the fragment from beneath my shirt. "But it has been broken. Do you know where we might find the rest of it?"

A collective shudder swept through the room, and several of the elders leapt to their feet, their teeth chattering wildly and their eyes wide with terror. "Evil!" one of the villagers cried out, pointing a shaky finger at me. "He bears the apocalypse stone!"

"So much death!" another wailed.

Only the wise woman remained calm, though she no longer graced me with a smile. "The amulet is a cursed thing," she spoke, her voice thick with sorrow."Cursed? How so?"

"It is a harbinger of death and destruction."

My chest tightened as if constricted by invisible hands. Leona and her men looked about in terror, unsure whether to take up arms. I lifted a hand to restrain them, then turned to the wise woman again.

"Please understand," I pleaded. "We had no knowledge of the amulet's dark past."

"But do you truly comprehend the depth of its power?" the wise woman asked sharply.

I took a deep breath, remembering the vision I'd received at Malachai's hand. Images flashed before me, conjured by the words of the wise woman's tale. I grasped the amulet tightly.

"We have no desire to wield it," I told her. "We wish to rid the world of it, once and for all."

The wise woman eyed me skeptically. "For that, you seek the other fragments?"

"Yes. Only when it has been fully reassembled can it be destroyed."

"And you are the only one who can destroy it."

"Yes," I answered. "But you knew that already, didn't you."

Her eyes bore into mine, searching for signs of deception. After a long moment, she finally nodded.

"You bear the apocalypse stone, yet your spirit remains pure. We will aid you." She turned to the elder who had escorted us to the village. "Take them to the temple."

"But wise one," he protested. "The curse—"

"Did you not hear our words? He is the one whose coming I have foreseen—the one who will rid the world of this threat forever."

"Or bring doom upon us all," one of the other elders muttered. The wise woman pretended not to hear him, and the chorus of hopeful whispers that rose around the hall seemed to indicate that his opinion was in the minority.

"What's happening?" Leona asked as the our guide rose reluctantly to his feet.

"I think they're about to take us to the next piece of the amulet," I answered.

We followed the village elder outside, past a small flock of chickens and a group of children playing in the dirt. Their wholesome laughter made me feel like I'd come home—or was that due to my uncanny resemblance to these people? In every way other than skin color, we seemed more alike than different. It was as though we shared a common ancestor, perhaps through my mother's side.

I laid these thoughts aside, though, as we took the path that led out of the village. The tribe gathered around us, forming something of an honor guard until after we'd passed the last hut. We left them behind us as we reached the winding path into the jungle.

"Stay close," Leona urged her men. They needed little encouragement. The air was thick and humid, and the jungle loomed like a lush green wall on either side of the path, hiding all sorts of potential dangers. Yet our guide strode confidently forward, as if he knew exactly the way to go.

"We're putting a lot of trust in these folks," Leona muttered. "If they're leading us into an ambush..."

"These people are peaceful," I rebuked her. "They're no danger to us."

"You're far too trusting, Samuel. I've known folks just as gentle who would slit their mother's throat for a piece of gold."

I didn't bother arguing with her. What was the point? I sensed that I had a deep and personal connection with these people. The story of their civilization's fall, of the shaggy-haired prophets who had wielded the ancient amulet—somehow, I sensed that it was my story, too. But how could I tell Leona all that?

We walked carefully through the jungle, shaded by the thick canopy overhead. The soft, mossy earth muted our steps, and we could barely hear the roar of the breakers on the beach. I took a deep breath and smelled the salty ocean breeze, mixed with something more elusive—a hint of ancient magic, perhaps. Though I knew I'd never smelled it, it tasted somehow familiar, just like everything else on this island.

At length, we emerged into a clearing. The peak of the island towered over us, the clouds tantalizingly close. At the center of the clearing stood an ancient stone temple. The ruins of other structures lay like fallen sentinels all around it, their smooth edges resembling the bony spine of the earth.

The elder led us to the door and motioned for us to wait. Leona and her men fidgeted anxiously, glancing every which way. But for me, the time passed easily. I stared up at the mountain peak, shrouded in the clouds, and once again felt that I'd come home.

The elder emerged from the temple and climbed carefully down the steep stairs. In his hands, he held the second fragment of the amulet.

"Behold the last relic of a fallen world," he said reverently. "Long ago, it brought death and destruction to our people. The last tidecaller entrusted it to us, to hold in safekeeping." He hesitated for a moment, then handed it to me. "If you are truly the one of whom the wise woman spoke, then the time of our stewardship has ended."

I graciously accepted the stone. As I fingered its cool, smooth surface, shivers ran down my spine and a low hum began to resonate through my ears. I could feel a grand vision coming upon me, much like the one I'd experienced back in Caravelia.

I closed my eyes as vivid images filled my mind, consuming me with their sheer intensity. I saw a rich, verdant land bathed in golden light. Shaggy-haired wizards ruled with an iron fist, their supreme power unquestioned. But their machinations were far above the concerns of the common people, who largely lived in peace.

I gasped as I saw myself among them. These were my ancestors, the ones who had created the amulet in order to keep their realm safe from any outside danger.

But then came the cataclysm, fire raining down from heaven and sinking the land beneath the waves. A few brave souls fought back against the chaos, reaching out to rescue the few who could be saved. They held off the darkness for a time, but they could not prevent the devastation from sweeping their world. When it was all over, only a few hundred survivors remained.

My heart raced as I realized that this was no mere story. This was history—*my* history. I was watching the fall of my people with my own eyes. And after their fall, my ancestors had been among those who had fought back against the darkness, only to be cast out by the survivors for crimes that had not been theirs.

The vision slowly faded, leaving me gasping for breath. Leona reached out to steady me.

"Are you all right?" she asked.

"I'm fine," I reassured her. "It's all making sense now."

"What's making sense? What do you mean?"

I briefly described my vision for her. The village elder waited patiently for me to finish before he spoke.

"If what you saw is true, then you are indeed descended from the great and terrible ones who brought this calamity upon us. That is why your powers flow from your shaggy hair."

Without thinking, I ran a hand through my unruly locks, contemplating the connection between myself and those who came before me. If my ancestors were truly responsible for bringing such a calamity upon their people, then perhaps destroying the amulet would allow me to make some restitution for their sins. Was that why I was the only one who could wield the power of the amulet? There had to be a reason why this artifact had chosen an obscure sea mage like me.

"Then it is my responsibility to rid the world of this cursed power, once and for all."

The village elder smiled. "Go, son of our people. May the spirits of our shared ancestors watch over you."

As if in answer, a wind blew through the trees, whispering through the leaves like the voices of those long lost. If I'd had the gift of clairvoyance, I had little doubt that I would have been able to sense their presence, just like the elder had said.

The jungle thinned out as we neared the beach, and the smell of saltwater mingled with the earthy petrichor of a recent light rain. Showers are frequent in the southern isles, and this one must have been gentle enough that we barely noticed it, shielded as we were by the thick jungle canopy.

"Farewell, great shaggy one," our native guide said as we reached the sand.

"Thank you," I said, bowing deeply. "Tell your wise woman that we will not rest until the amulet has been destroyed."

The guide returned to the shadows of the jungle. In just a few steps, he had completely disappeared from our view.

Crabs skittered across the damp sand as we strode out toward our launch. Leona walked smartly, her hand resting on the hilt of her sword. Off in the distance, we could see the gleaming white sails and the glistening black sides of the *Ebony Eagle*.

"Samuel," Leona hissed, stopping suddenly. "Do you feel something?"

I frowned. "Like what?"

In an instant, her sword was in her hands. She spun and quickly scanned the jungle. Something had spooked her, and true to form, she looked like she intended to get the jump on them first.

But when they came, it wasn't with swords, but with sorcery.

A sudden chill ran down my spine, and I stumbled, holding onto a sturdy tree for support. The pieces of the amulet tucked under my shirt grew warm against my skin, as if someone were calling for it, and the world began to tilt and spin all around me.

Binding spell! I realized. It felt the same as the spell the cultists had used on me in Malachai's hidden enclave.

I cast a protective ward, nullifying its effects. Scarcely had I done so before figures emerged from the shadows, clothed in long, black robes. Carved runes glowed from the wooden staves they held.

"Form a circle!" Leona shouted. Her crew rallied to her call, and just as swiftly, the cultists surrounded us, cutting off our escape.

My heart raced. The effects of the binding spell were dissipating, but we were outnumbered. How had they found us? Had they been following us from the beginning?

Instead of attacking, the cultists took up a chant. The air around us grew thick, and a cloud of darkness seemed to overshadow us.

"The circle!" I shouted, suddenly realizing that they were using our own formation against us. Sure enough, the ground beneath our feet seemed to glow, reminding me of the chalk circle on the floor in Malachai's hideout.

"To me, boys!" Leona shouted. Taking up a battle cry, her men lunged forward in an effort to break out. Immediately, the spell was broken, and the cultists began to stagger back.

But they weren't surprised for long. Although we had the initiative, their staves had a wider reach than our swords. We wounded three of them before they began to push us back, swinging at us mightily with their staves. Soon, they'd forced us back into a circle, and the chanting began anew.

"Why do you resist us?" a disembodied voice whispered in my ear. "Join us, Samuel. It is your destiny."

"Sam!" Leona shouted. "Do something!"

Her words snapped me out of my daze. I clutched the fragmented amulet to my chest, drawing on its power for strength as I had when trapped in the shipwreck. A sudden burst of magical energy surged through my body, a primal force that demanded to be used. I lifted my free hand.

"By the locks of my ancestors, begone!"

The effect was immediate. The cultists' staves shattered, and they were flung back into the jungle like rag-dolls. Their dark spells crumbled like glass against the rocks.

"To me!" Leona shouted again.

We ran for our lives, fully expecting the cultists to rally for a counterattack. For a moment, I feared that they'd stranded us, but the launch was exactly where we'd left it. Our men quickly surrounded it, and soon we were hauling it back to the water.

"Cover us, Sam!" Leona ordered. I turned, holding my hand out, but the cultists were nowhere to be seen.

"This isn't the last time," the disembodied voice whispered in my ear. "We will meet each other again."

Once again, chills ran down my back. I scrambled aboard the launch with the others, and together we rowed back to the ship.

"Safe," breathed Leona, sheathing her sword.

"Aye," I said hopefully, slumping into the bottom of the launch. But inwardly, I knew I would never be safe until the amulet was completely destroyed.

In Which I Ride the Wild Dolphins as We Narrowly Escape the Cultists Again

The tropical waters of the Cerulean Sea are generally more placid than our northerly waters, but they still receive their fair share of squalls, storms, and other disturbances. In fact, the hurricanes down south can be downright frightening, enough to challenge even the most powerful sea mage.

Thankfully, the storm we encountered was much weaker than a hurricane, though it did churn the waters quite violently. The *Ebony Eagle* cut through the turbulent waves like a knife, accompanied by dolphins playfully leaping off our bow. They seemed to care nothing for the dark clouds massing above us, frolicking ahead of our wake.

"Sam!" Leona shouted from the helm, squinting against the spray. "Ease up the pressure on the mainmast! Quick now!"

"Aye, Captain," I called back, lifting my hands for the spell. I traced the ancient glyphs in the air, holding back the wind just enough to fill our sails without tipping us over or putting too much strain on the mast.

"Good work," Leona said absent-mindedly, her eyes on the waters ahead as she expertly shifted expertly her weight with the rolling surf. "Isadora would be puking her guts out in this squall."

"What was that?"

"I said, Isadora would be puking her guts out in this squall," Leona repeated, louder this time. "That woman couldn't handle half the rough water we've encountered."

"Come now, Leona," I said in a soothing tone. "Let's not dwell on her any more than we have to."

"Don't you get it, Sam?" she said, ignoring my suggestion. "Isadora is just as much an enemy to us as those cultists. For them, it's about getting the amulet, but for it's a personal vendetta for her."

"Are you sure? For all we know, she isn't thinking about you at all."

"I wouldn't bet on it. I know that traitorous wench as well as if she were my sister—which she was, in a certain sense." She spat over the edge of the railing—an impressive feat, from where she stood.

I sighed heavily, knowing there was no use arguing. Still, I couldn't just let her brood on the subject and ignore everything else.

"Isadora isn't nearly as dangerous as Malachai," I said aloud.

"She's not half the privateer I am, of course," said Leona, relaxing her grip on the helm somewhat and clearly not listening to me anymore. "You can see it in the eyes of her men. Don't you agree?"

"Uh..."

"I always say, you can judge a good captain by the quality of her men. When the boys are willing to give their lives for her, you know she's top-notch." Leona threw her head back and laughed. "Can't see any of her ragged, motley crew doing that, can you?"

"Well, I certainly see Malachai's followers giving up their lives," I said, trying to change the subject.

She pondered this for a moment, then nodded. "Good point. Isadora's probably working with the cultists—hell, she may even secretly be one of them."

I inwardly groaned. This was not the change of topic I'd had in mind. But Leona was so single-mindedly fixated on her rival that even a discussion of the weather would invoke her name—as indeed, it already had.

"Maybe we should just focus on finding the next fragment of the amulet, instead of worrying about Isadora," I said, trying a direct approach.

"What exactly do you think I'm doing, Sam?" Leona argued. "If Isadora is part of the cult, then maybe she knows something we don't. If we play our cards right, she could lead us right to that third fragment."

I rolled my eyes. "Come on, Leona. Do you really believe that Isadora is a cultist?"

"Of course I do. Why else would she be after the amulet? She's already betrayed me once. She'll do practically anything for power."

I shook my head, unconvinced. Isadora might be ruthless and clever, but a cultist? She seemed too independently minded, too confident and sure of herself to let a strong-willed leader like Malachai bend her to his ways.

The winds and waves continued to rage around us, forcing me to channel my magic again. Chanting softly, I cast an aura of calm around us. The waves crashed against our little bubble with ferocity, but my magic held strong, pushing back against the squall's petulant fury.

"Well, Sam? What do you think?"

"I suppose it's possible," I admitted, more to end the discussion than anything else. But Leona wouldn't let it die.

"It's certain," she said firmly. "I'm telling you, Sam, she wants that amulet. I can see it in her eyes. She wants it just as much as Malachai—perhaps even more. And if that doesn't prove she's a part of his cult, I don't know what will."

"Captain!" the lookout shouted. "Ship approaching!"

"What sort?" Leona called back.

"I can't rightly tell. Her sails are all furled, and she's sitting so low in the water I can barely see her."

Leona and I exchanged a knowing look. Maybe it was nothing more than a local fishing boat—but in this squall? We were far enough from the nearest trade routes that it couldn't be a passing merchant, and as for Soren and the *Black Sword*—

Suddenly, the squall grew into a tempest. Clouds swirled above us, and lighting flashed overhead. The waves, which had been only rocky, began to surge with enough power to throw us to our knees.

"Sam!" Leona shouted. "There's sorcery in this storm!"

She was right. Whoever was in that other ship, their sea mage was much more powerful than me. I channeled more magic into the aura of calm that I'd cast, turning it into a shield, but I doubted I'd last very long against such an onslaught.

"Can we outrun them?" I shouted.

"Maybe," Leona answered. "How long can you hold out?"

"I don't know. Not long, at this rate."

"Then we'll turn and fight." She turned to her men and began to bark orders. "Come on, you sea dogs! Let's show these fools how we fight in the Azure Sea!"

The crew immediately sprang into action. Archers strung their bows and took position along the railing. I spared a bit of effort from the shield to cast a few spells of enhancement over them, then peered from my perch atop the aftcastle as the enemy ship crested the next wave.

It was as unlike our vessel as a crow is to a hawk. Instead of curving gracefully from a sleek and slender aftcastle to a proud, defiant bow, the other ship was long and flat, and her hull came to an ugly vertical peak on either side. Her mast—if you could call it that—was a single stubby trunk with a large sail furled below a yard that was far too wide. But her primary means of propulsion was not the sail. Dozens of oars jutted out on either side of her, swinging together in mesmerizing unison, cutting into the water and pushing her against the waves.

A ship like that didn't need any windcasting to propel it. All the sea mage had to do was cast a strengthening spell over the poor sods chained to their oars, leaving him free to focus his attention—

and magical might—on whatever enemy lay before them.

And as the enemy longboat—for that was the only way to describe it—came nearer, I saw my opponent standing calmly at the bow. He was a tall, lean figure with long, dark hair, and eyes that seemed to glow with power. From this distance, I could tell that the other crew was made up of Malachai's cultists, but instead of the dark brown robes they wore, the sea mage's robes were light gray. He raised his hands and summoned a lightning bolt, which I barely managed to deflect with my magic.

"What do you see, Sam?" Leona called.

"It's the cultists," I answered uneasily. "And they have a powerful sorcerer on board. Perhaps we're making a mistake."

"Prepare for battle!" she barked, ignoring my misgivings.

My heart hammered as I summoned all the power I could. Arcane words, ancient and powerful, flowed from my lips in a steady stream. But just as I was forming the beginnings of my attack, a fierce and potent counter-spell unraveled all my efforts.

"What was that, Sam?"

"He countered my spell. I'm telling you, we're making a mistake!"

Leona scowled. "Is that all you've got? No more tricks up your sleeve?"

"Hold steady," I growled, clenching my teeth. With a deep breath, I summoned my power again, this time striking out before the enemy had a chance to negate it. But instead of directly countering my spell, he simply uttered a low, guttural chant and lifted his hands to deflect my attack into the boiling sea.

"It's no use," I shouted. "We've got to get out of here!"

I couldn't imagine how the cultists had gotten ahold of a ship like this. Until now, I'd thought they were little more than a secret society parasitically leeching off the noble houses of Caravelia. I'd told myself that they might extend to a few of the neighboring kingdoms, at most. Fielding a warship required far more resources than I'd thought they had.

But now was not the time to dwell on such thoughts. As Leona turned us about, I filled our sails with wind, making the wooden timbers creak in protest. The *Eagle* surged forward, pulling ahead with the cultists following close on our tail.

Arrows suddenly began to fall on the deck. With the wind at our back, the enemy's range was much farther than our own, putting us in danger.

"Sam!" Leona shouted.

"On it," I answered, turning to deflect the next volley. But the cult's sorcerer was enhancing their shots, and the arrows fell among us like lead, unaffected by the winds.

Screams went up from our crew as they began to take wounds from the onslaught. Our own archers tried to shoot back, but with the tailwind, it was no use.

"Use the amulet, Sam!" Leona urged.

I clutched the two fragments of the amulet beneath my shirt, drawing power from them. The sudden surge of energy caught me off guard. The next volley of arrows exploded in midair, shattering into splinters and sawdust. The enemy sorcerer shook his fists in rage.

"Ha!" said Leona, grinning exultantly. "That'll show them!"

But my mind was elsewhere. With the burst of power from the amulet, I suddenly became aware of the exact location of the third fragment. And what was more, it wasn't far.

"I know where to find the amulet!" I shouted over the howling of the wind.

"What?" Leona shouted back.

"The amulet," I answered, coming closer so that she could hear. "I know where to find the third fragment. It's hidden in a lagoon, three leagues from here."

"Why didn't you say so sooner?" Leona asked. She glanced over her shoulder at the pursuing cultists. "Time to lose our tail."

"Aye," I agreed, drawing a sharp breath. The enemy archers were no longer shooting at us, but their ship was still in close pursuit. As I watched, they unfurled their blood-red sail and surged forward, oars straining to give them an extra boost. On their deck, I caught the glint of steel.

"Uh oh," I said. "Leona, we're about to have boarders!"

"I just had an idea. Look!"

I turned to where she was pointing. A sunken island loomed just off our bow, vanishing with the swells. I reached out with my magic and saw that it was actually a reef, surrounding a sunken atoll. Any captain would be a fool to sail his ship into its sharp crags and treacherous currents.

"Are you crazy?" I asked in disbelief. "We'll never make it through there! And even if we do, they'll just follow us! I don't know if you've noticed, but they've got a *significantly* shallower draft than the *Eagle*."

Leona just threw back her head and laughed, making my stomach sink. "Ease up just a bit," Leona commanded. "Let them gain on us."

"But Leona, they've got grappling hooks!"

"Excellent! Now do as I say!"

I bit my lip and eased back on the wind, letting the longboat draw closer. Our archers began to shoot at them, and they returned fire, forcing me to channel more of my magic toward deflection.

A grappling hook flew through the air, guided by the invisible hand of their sea mage's sorcery. It snagged on the railing just behind us.

"They've got us!" I told her. "Leona, what should I do?"

"Let them do it again," she urged.

Another hook landed, and another. The cultists were only a few moments from pulling alongside us. Their warriors waited eagerly on the deck of the longboat, some wielding runic staffs, others wearing fearsome masks and brandishing swords and short blades. I had no doubt they would kill everyone on the *Eagle* except for me.

"Leona?"

"Give us wind, now!" she shouted, gripping the helm with whitened knuckles.

I didn't need to be told twice. With arrows falling all around us, I called forth a mighty gale, sending us careening through the reefs.

"Thread a course, Sam," Leona told me. I swallowed, but there was no time to object. She didn't have magic to see all the dangers like I did, which meant that she was relying on me to get us through. But still, she commanded the helm, which meant that the ship responded to her. If she and I inadvertently went at cross purposes, we were liable to be wrecked on the rocks.

The lines on the grappling hooks went taut as we began to tow the longboat behind us. I closed my eyes and focused on the path ahead, using my magic to watch for obstacles. My awareness expanded, as if the ship itself became an extension of my own body. The sea foam rolled dangerously off the reefs, but miraculously, we threaded a narrow path through.

Unfortunately, so did the cultists.

"On my command," Leona said softly, "I want you to turn us hard to starboard. Do you understand?"

An arrow whistled past my ear. The men on the deck were screaming, but there was little we could do for them now. I nodded.

"Steady," she muttered as we sped through the relative calm at the center of the atoll. Another arrow embedded itself in the helm next to Leona's hand, but she didn't even flinch.

I hazarded a glance behind us. The cultists were chanting now, eager to fight.

"Steady."

The reef on the other side loomed before us. Just ahead lay a ridge that was mostly hidden under the surf. It would surely be fatal for us, but was it shallow enough to damage the longboat?

"Now!"

The yards on the mast swung hard as I channeled a powerful burst of wind to our starboard. Leona turned the wheel, and we made the sharpest turn I think I've ever felt while at sea. The longboat whipped past us, their oars lifted high in the air. Too late, they saw the danger. Their longboat shattered against the reef, men falling overboard as their hull turned to splinters. A resounding cheer went up from our men.

"Steady!" Leona shouted. "We're not through it yet!"

She didn't need to tell me that. With the cultists off our tail, though, I could channel all my energy into guiding us safely through. Their archers fired a few pot shots, but soon we were out of range, leaving them shipwrecked behind us.

As soon as the sunken atoll was safely behind us, I collapsed to the deck.

"You okay there, Sam?"

"I'm fine," I stammered. "I just... need a minute."

Leona smirked, her crew still cheering all around us. "Took the wind out of you, did it?"

"Aye," I said, closing my eyes. The amulet felt unbearably heavy around my neck, as if its power was too much for me to bear. And perhaps that wasn't far from the truth. But even as I lay exhausted on the deck, I could sense the third fragment calling to me from the next atoll, only a few leagues away.

***

As we sailed away from the sunken atoll, the winds suddenly took a turn for the worse, as if mother nature herself were bent on keeping us from finding the next fragment.

"Watch those cross-winds," Leona called out as the squall threatened to blow us off course. "Can you give us a bearing, Sam?"

"Thirty degrees to port, Captain," I told her. Though the weather was clearly worsening, I didn't want to cast a calming spell just yet. With the cultists still potentially on our tail, speed was of paramount importance.

Suddenly, the squall turned into a violent tempest, transforming the sea into a maelstrom. Fierce winds whipped the waves into frothy white peaks, nearly drowning out Leona's voice as she barked orders to her men. Her ebony braid whipped around her face, and her hands gripped the wheel with iron determination.

"Brace yourselves!" she shouted over the deafening roar of the storm. Rain suddenly poured down in sheets, drenching us all to the bone.

I used all my magic to try and create a bubble of peace for our ship, but there was something in the tempest that resisted my efforts. Was it the cultists? Or merely some forgotten curse on these waters themselves?

Just when I thought we had the upper hand, Leona's frantic voice cut through the howling winds. Her eyes were wide as she pointed to an obstruction just off our bow, and when I saw it, my stomach dropped through the deck. We were sailing into the heart of a massive whirlpool, a monstrous and sorcerous maw that defied all logic.

"By the gods, new and old..."

"Get us out of here, Sam!"

I closed my eyes and reached deep within myself, tapping into the deepest wells of my magical gift. My scalp itched and tingled as I created a counter-current to push against the whirlpool's pull. The strain was excruciating, like a thousand hot needles digging into my skull. But between my spells and the crew's effort, the *Ebony Eagle* soon veered away from the looming danger.

"That was too close," Leona gasped as we narrowly avoided the churning waters. Where that unholy whirlpool would have taken us, I had no idea.

"Aye," I said, glancing up at the sky. As suddenly and ferociously as it had come upon us, the squall suddenly let up. I reached out with my magic and sensed that there was something sorcerous in the maelstrom, even more chaotic and ancient than dark magic. It was a good thing we had managed to avoid it.

But as we pulled away, I sensed that we had company.

"Look," I said, pointing off toward the horizon. As the clouds gradually parted, we saw another longboat rowing parallel to our course.

"Persistent vermin," Leona spat. "Will they stop at nothing?"

I narrowed my eyes and grasped the incomplete amulet under my shirt. Something wasn't right—if the cultists wanted to attack, why were they running parallel and not trying to intercept? That only made sense if—

"They're not after us," I blurted aloud. "They're after the other piece of the amulet—there, up ahead."

We turned and saw the white sandy beaches and low, tree-filled islands of a large atoll up ahead. A few rocks projected from the sea, shielding the lagoon where the third fragment of the amulet lay.

"We've got to beat them," I told Leona. "If they get the fragment before we do—"

"I know, Sam," Leona snapped. "But we'll be sitting ducks out there, especially if they have any more ships around."

She was right, of course. At the rate we were going, the best we could hope was to reach the lagoon at the same time as the cultists' longboat. And who knew how many more were already in pursuit? Even if we somehow managed to beat them, we would still have to spend time searching for the fragment of the amulet, time the cultists could use to set up a blockade and trap us there.

Or would we? I clutched the partially assembled amulet to my chest and realized that I knew exactly where the third fragment was. I sensed it so surely that I could guide an arrow to it. Of course, we would need something much larger than an arrow if we were to reclaim it. If only we could launch something that a person could ride—

A dolphin breached the waters off our bow. The squall had temporarily driven off their pod, but they were back now, swimming and playing alongside us. Suddenly, an idea dawned on me.

"Uh, Sam?" Leona asked as I pulled off my shirt. "What are you doing?"

"Stay out here and circle the island," I told her. "Better yet, try to create a diversion to keep those cultists busy. But keep as much distance as you can."

"What in the name of the gods are you up to?"

"I'm going for the amulet. Just trust me."

There was no time to waste. Leona shouted after me as I ran toward the bow, but without looking back, I jumped over the railing and dove into the waters just ahead of our wake.

The dolphins scattered, making me fear that my idea wouldn't work. I channeled my magic to keep pace with the ship, but it was hard work, both physically and magically. I couldn't keep it up for long. After a short while, though, the animals' natural curiosity got the best of them, and they came closer to see what this strange, pink-skinned creature was.

That's right, I thought silently, willing them to come closer. *Just a little more... that's right, a little more...*

Have you ever ridden a wild horse? I can't say that I have. Being a sailor all my life, the only horses I've ridden have been thoroughly tame. But I can say I've ridden a wild dolphin, which is probably no less crazy.

The first few minutes were the wildest. The dolphin bucked and swerved, breaching and diving in its efforts to cast me off. If not for my magic, I certainly would have drowned. But letting my hair flow wild in the waters all around us, I reached out and soothed it as best I could.

"There, girl," I whispered, willing it to understand me. "I'm not here to hurt you; I just need a little help."

Surprisingly, the dolphin began to calm down. As the rest of the pod chattered and squawked alongside us, she slowed and looked up at me with one small, beady eye.

"That's right," I said, sensing her curiosity. "I need your help to find the other piece of this."

I've been told that horses are intelligent creatures, but I suspect that dolphins are ten times more so. When I held up the amulet, it shimmered in the shallow waters, and the dolphins all began chattering anew. Suddenly, it seemed that they had all accepted me, including the one I was clinging to. In fact, I sensed that she was even a little proud that I had chosen her.

"That's right," I said, patting her. "Now, let's go."

We took off like an arrow, quickly leaving the *Ebony Eagle* behind. I clutched the amulet tightly with one hand as I clung to the dolphin's dorsal fin with the other. The rest of the pod went ahead, helping us to ride their wake, and in no time, we were in the shallow waters of the atoll, surrounded by gorgeous reefs and shining white sands.

"That way," I said, willing my dolphin steed in the direction of the third fragment. I couldn't see it yet, but I could sense it like a beacon on a dark night. Keeping my eyes locked forward, I guided us in until we were right over it.

The shipwreck where I'd found the first fragment had been relatively well-preserved on the bottom of the sea. But here, all that remained were a few shattered timbers. But in the heart of the wreckage lay a small chest, buried almost completely under the sand. I quickly dug it out and pried the lid off with my knife. Sure enough, the third fragment of the amulet lay inside.

The ride back took a little persuading. Wild dolphins may be intelligent, but they're fickle, temperamental creatures. But when I set out on my own, ignoring them, it was too much for them to handle. The pod quickly swam to me, like children who could not bear being ignored, and carried me back outside the lagoon.

I arrived none too soon, since the *Ebony Eagle* didn't stand a chance against the cultists' sorcery without a skilled mage. They must have guessed my intentions when they saw me swim off with the dolphins, since they had turned away from the atoll and were now bearing down on the *Eagle*. Our archers were already taking up positions when Leona hauled me aboard.

"Have you got it?" she asked.

I gasped for breath and held it up for an answer. A single curt nod, and she turned to her men.

"All right, you sea dogs! Let's give these boys the slip!"

In no time at all, I was back on the upper deck, filling our sails as we pulled away. I drew on the power of the amulet to summon a thick fog, which quickly enveloped our pursuers. It would take some time for their sorcerers to dispel it, and by then, we would be well on our way.

"Ha!" Leona laughed in appreciation. "That'll keep them occupied."

"Right," I said, gasping for breath. My heart pounded in my chest at the exhaustion and exhilaration of our narrow escape.

"You've done well, Sam. But keep your spells ready. We're not out of their grasp yet."

"How is it that they're always only one or two steps behind us?" I pondered aloud. "It's almost like they're reading our minds with their magic."

Leona raised an eyebrow. "Are they?"

"No. Of course not. But they wouldn't need to, if—"

"If we have a traitor in our midst," Leona finished my thought. "We'll have to look into that before we go after the final piece of the amulet."

"Right," I said, holding it before me. The third piece fit seamlessly into the others, but there was still a large gap for the last fragment. Our journey was far from over.

In Which We Lose the Amulet and Very Nearly Our Lives, As Well

I wasn't looking forward to confronting Soren. Where I was a dropout and a wanderer, he was one of the most promising young captains in the King's Fleet. And yet, neither Leona nor I could ignore how the cultists had attacked when Soren's crew should have been protecting our flank. No one on the *Ebony Eagle* could have had a hand in that. It had to be someone from the Fleet.

We sighted the *Black Sword* the next day and signaled to them with our flags that we needed to talk. I reached instinctively for the partially assembled amulet, but it was still in the chest in my quarters. It was just as well, since I doubted I would need it soon. As much as I relished the power it gave me, I was getting to the point where I didn't need it on my immediate person to tap into its power. I just needed it in my general possession.

As our ships pulled in close enough for our voices to carry, I leaned over the edge of the railing, using my magic to amplify my voice.

"Ahoy, Soren!"

"Ahoy!" he called from the upper deck of the *Sword*. I couldn't help but note that his voice carried just as well as mine, without any magical amplification.

"Come up alongside us," I replied. "We need to parley!"

"Parley?"

"You heard him right, you preening buffoon!" Leona called out to him.

We watched as Soren's majestic frigate approached our smaller, more agile ship. As they turned to pull the *Eagle,* Leona shouted orders at the crew while I fine-tuned my windcasting. It was a tricky maneuver, but working with practiced efficiency, our crews managed to secure the two ships together with thick cords. We furled our sails and drifted while Soren crossed the narrow plank.

"Soren," I said coolly, nodding as he came aboard.

"Samuel." He glanced around the ship, then gestured with his eyes to the aftcastle. "Your cabin, I presume, Captain Black?"

"Of course," Leona replied, leading the way.

As soon as the door shut behind us, we dropped all pretense of friendliness. "How did they find us?" Leona asked, glaring daggers.

Soren raised an eyebrow. "How did who find you?"

"The cultists back at the atolls—two longboats full of them. You're supposed to be our escort. How did they get past you?"

For an instant, he let his mask fall, and his eyes flared in rage before turning to shards of ice again.

"Are you questioning my competence?"

Leona scoffed. "I'm not *questioning* anything. Sam can attest to what we saw, if you doubt me."

"I wouldn't ask a washed-up sea mage like Samuel to attest to anything," Soren said contemptuously.

"Enough of this," I said, stepping between them. "Soren, Captain Black asked you a question. What is your answer?"

He pointedly ignored me, meeting Leona's steely gaze with his own. "I don't know," he said slowly.

"Don't know what? How those cultists found us, or how they got past you??"

"I swear, I have no idea!" Soren roared.

I paused. He seemed genuine enough, and the enemy's sorcery was powerful enough that they could have slipped by him unnoticed. But that didn't explain how they'd known where we were.

Leona folded her arms, diffusing some of the tension. "If it wasn't you, then it must have been someone else. One of your lieutenants, perhaps."

"Are you saying there's an informant in our ranks?"

She glared at him as if to ask: *Are you stupid?*

Soren took a deep breath, regaining his cool. "We shall investigate this matter at once. Thank you for bringing this to my attention, Captain Black."

"And how long with it take for this 'investigation' to provide us with answers?" she asked, rolling her eyes. "Will it be before the cultists have struck again?"

"You appear to be in disagreement with my intended course of action," Soren said, glaring back at her, his cold eyes aflame. "What would you suggest as an alternative?"

"That you sail your 'escort' back to Caravelia. We never asked for you to join us. Get out of our way and let us fulfill the mission King Leander gave us."

"What about the cultists? Now that we know that Malachai has a fleet—"

"If you aren't there to fight them off, what good are you?" Leona bellowed. "Just leave! I don't care where you go. Just let us be. *That's* how you can get rid of the informant among your ranks!"

For several tense moments, Soren only stared at her. Then, his back ramrod straight, he slowly rose to his feet. "If that is how it must be, Captain Black, then I will acquiesce to your demands. I only wish that you provide them to me in writing, so that I have proof for the king when he asks why I abandoned you."

"Fine," Leona growled. She grabbed the nearest sheet of parchment and scribbled a note on it, dripping ink in her fury. "Will this suffice?"

"It will require your seal, as well."

"To hell with it," she cursed, pulling a ring from one of her fingers. She thrust it into his chest along with the ink-spattered parchment. "If they question who gave it to you, show them this."

Soren drew a sharp breath and bowed. "Good day, Captain Black. I hope we shall meet again someday under more... amiable circumstances."

"Get off my ship."

I closed the door softly after he left, staring at it for a few moments as I clenched and unclenched my fists. Soren's presence had left a bitter taste in my mouth, but I tried to put that out of my mind as I turned to face Leona.

"Well," I said, "that could have gone worse."

"Or better," she grumbled, collapsing onto her chair. "Do you believe he's telling the truth?"

"I don't know," I admitted. "Something's not sitting right with me, but that could just be my history with Soren tainting my judgment. We joined the King's Fleet at around the same time, you know."

"Yes," Leona mused. "But I think you're right. There's something fishy about the whole affair, almost as if..."

I frowned, a thought suddenly occurring to me. "As if he's the informant?"

"Yes, in fact. Exactly like that."

"That's not likely. Why would Soren throw his career away? He's got a lot more to lose than I do."

"Are you sure?"

Her question took me aback. Soren, a cultist? No—that was crazy. Or was it? A feeling of dread suddenly gripped me. I reached out for the amulet, calling upon its power, but instead I felt only an emptiness. My eyes widened in shock, and my stomach began to churn.

"Oh, no!"

I took off at a run, bolting down the hall toward my quarters.

"Sam!" Leona called. "What's going on?"

But I couldn't stop to answer. Not when so much was at stake.

I threw open the door to my cabin, fearing the worst. My chest lay open in the center of the room, not against the side of the hull where I had left it. The lock had been forcefully broken open.

"Oh, no," I groaned, staring into it. Sure enough, the amulet was gone.

I frantically pulled out clothing and other personal belongings, vainly searching for it among the debris. *I've just misplaced it,* I told myself. *And I forgot that I'd left the chest out.* But deep down, I knew that was wrong.

Footsteps in the hallway outside snapped me out of my panic. "Samuel! What is going on?" Leona asked from the doorway. When she saw the empty chest and my belongings strewn across the floor, her face hardened to stone.

"The amulet," I stammered, barely managing to speak. "It's—"

"Gone," she finished. "How?"

I struggled to find the words, mentally kicking myself for my stupidity. Why hadn't I kept the amulet with me? My scrimshaw family locket or the scrystone compass—they were things I should have stored in my chest. And why hadn't I thought to put the amulet in the hidden compartment in the lid? If only I'd been more cautious—

"Spit it out, Sam," Leona commanded, kneeling beside me. "What's happened?"

"The amulet," I finally managed. "It's gone. Soren..."

Leona swore under her breath. "That slimy eel... Well, don't just sit there. Come on!"

I followed her wordlessly back to the deck, still stunned by the loss. Had Soren truly betrayed us?

But why would he throw away such a promising career with the fleet? Unless...

My cheeks blanched, and my stomach fell out beneath me. Soren must have been in league with the cult from the beginning. Even as Leona shouted orders, a sharp cry sounded from the lookout above.

"Longboats, Captain! Two of them!"

I gripped the railing and peered over the side. Sure enough, by two of the cultists' longboats had joined Soren's ship alongside us. Archers lined the decks of all three ships, and clouds of dark sorcery swirled above them.

"Damnation!" Leona shouted as the archers loosed the first volley. "Sam!"

"On it!"

I lifted my hands and hastily sent out a blast of wind, deflecting most of the arrows in midair. But I wasn't in time to stop all of them, and several fell among us, wounding a few men on the deck and in the rigging. One of them screamed as he fell into the sea, while the rest quickly scrambled for cover as best they could.

The cultists loosed another volley, aided by sorcery. I recognized the mage of the nearest ship as the man who had followed us in our race to recover the third fragment of the amulet. But this time, I was ready. Instead of windcasting to deflect the arrows, I cast a magical barrier, slowing the arrows in midflight and dropping them into the sea.

"Good work, Sam!" Leona shouted encouragingly.

I gasped for breath, my scalp tingling. The spell had taken more energy than I had expected. At this rate, how much longer could I hold them off? With the second longboat and Soren's own mage, it was three against one—and I no longer had the power of the amulet to call upon.

Our archers returned fire, but after seeing how easily the enemy mages deflected their arrows, I decided to save my strength.

"Sam!" Leona shouted from the upper deck. "Give us some wind!"

As the cultists loosed a third volley, I sent a mighty blast of wind into our sails. The *Ebony Eagle* leaped forward, timbers creaking under the strain. Our men sought cover as the arrows fell behind us, only a few of them striking the stern-most parts of our deck. Leona stood defiantly amidst the onslaught.

"Secure that line!" she shouted, pointing with her sword. "Hold the yards steady! And you there—ready a patch for that sail!"

I quickly climbed to the aft deck and peered back at our enemy. Soren's frigate had fallen behind, but the cultists' longboats were gaining on us, as if the slaves who manned the oars had been strengthened by uncanny sorcery. It seemed that we were repeating our previous fight all over again, but with two enemy ships on our tail instead of one.

"Any ideas, Sam?" Leona asked.

"I don't know. The amulet—"

"Damn the amulet! We need to lose these creeps!"

I looked ahead and saw the whirlpool looming off our bow. The lagoon had to be nearby, though the rough waters and constant spray made it difficult to see where the land lay.

"Whirlpool, Captain!" the lookout cried.

"Head into it!" Leona shouted, undeterred. "They'd be crazy to follow us, wouldn't they?"

"Not as crazy as us," I muttered nervously. But my words only made her laugh.

"Come on, Sam! You'll see us through, won't you?"

An idea suddenly struck me. "Hang on!" I shouted, throwing caution to the wind as I lifted my hands to channel a powerful gale.

The wind nearly tore the sails off, pulling us forward with such sudden force that it nearly snapped the mast. But more importantly, the winds whipped up the waves all around us, churning the sea into a mighty spray. I channeled that spray into a fine mist, casting spells of obfuscation as we descended into the funnel.

Arrows fell all around us, quivering as they struck our deck. Too late, I realized that the cultists had loosed another volley—and this time, they were using fire arrows. The crew shouted as one of our sails caught fire, whipping frantically in the wind. Elsewhere, the flaming pitch began to sear the deck as men scrambled to put out the flames.

"Sam!" Leona shouted.

But we had already descended into the whirlpool, taxing my powers to the utmost. Between the swirling waves of the maelstrom's maw rising to crush us and the flames rapidly spreading throughout the ship, it was hard to say which was the more immediate threat.

Thinking quickly, I drew upon my magic to multiply the mists, hoping that Leona's men would do the rest. The wind now carried enough moisture to thoroughly soak the ship, putting out the worst of the fires. But it also made the deck slick, and several of the crew hung on for dear life as the whirlpool began to pull us around.

"Secure the sails, you sea dogs!" Leona shouted as she wrestled with the helm. "Steady now—steady!"

As she swung the helm to pull us out of the maelstrom, I had just enough presence of mind to turn the wind crossways, sufficient to pull us out. Our sails, singed by the flames, began to tear loose in the wind, but the mainsail held steady just long enough to get us clear.

"Land ho!" the lookout cried as we surged into the shallow lagoon. We had only a few moments of warning before we ran aground with an awful lurch.

I staggered and fell to the deck. For a very brief moment, I feared that we'd been wrecked against the rocky reef. But it seemed we had merely been beached by the low tide. The ship was tipping dangerously, but the hull still held.

"Lower the sails!" Leona shouted, gripping my shoulder tightly. "Sam—kill the wind!"

"On it," I told her. I used my magic to deflect the wind all around us, still keeping it high enough to churn up a mist. But instead of propelling us, it now only served to hide us.

I rose to my feet and peered back toward the water. Now was the moment of truth, where we'd see how well my spells of obfuscation would hold. Against two dark sorcerers, I feared the worst—and indeed, for a terrifying moment, I thought I saw the prow of one of the longboats emerging from the mists. But it soon became clear that it was just my imagination.

"Drop the sails and lower the yards," Leona shouted. "Give them no more sign than we have to. Sam, can you hide us?"

"Already done," I told her, though I cast another spell for good measure. "From out there, all they should see is the lagoon."

She grunted. "Good work. That ought to hold them until the tide carries us out of here."

"I hope so, Leona. They're still out there searching, though. It won't take them long to find out where we've gone."

"Let them search," Leona said defiantly. "The next time, we'll be ready for them, won't we?"

I nodded as confidently as I could manage. But without the power of the amulet, I was anything but sure.

In Which Our Morale and Efforts are Bolstered By an Unlikely Defector

Thankfully, the *Ebony Eagle* was merely beached. She'd return to action as soon as the tide came in. I had laid multiple concealing spells on our flight from Soren and his cultist conspirators, but we still had to stay vigilant. The longboats they employed were more than capable of gliding into the shallow lagoon to take us. And since they would almost certainly hide their approach with their own magic, it fell upon me to climb to the highest point in the atoll—a large rocky outcropping—and keep watch until high tide.

The waves crashed against the rocks below me, sending up a fine saltwater spray that soaked my hair and beard. Below me in the lagoon, the crew carried out their orders in hushed tones, as if speaking too loudly might betray us. And truthfully, there was a chance it could. I wrapped my fingers tightly around my mother's locket, feeling reassured by its familiar shape and texture as I turned my gaze to the sea.

An unexpected movement on the beach caught my attention. A lone figure staggered up from the water, her dark red hair clinging to her head like seaweed. Her black robes were soaked, as if she'd been swimming in them, but they were so long and heavy that they made her look as out of place as a cultist in the heart of Caravelia—or perhaps in our little lagoon.

I tensed immediately, narrowing my eyes. How had she gotten past my watch? Had she swum from as far out as the whirlpool? I reluctantly began to summon my magic, knowing that I should dispatch her before she discovered our hiding place, but something stayed my hand. Did I know her? As she came closer, I noticed that she looked strangely familiar...

With a start, I realized I *had* seen her before—in the vision from the scrystone compass, before Malachai had abducted me. I hurriedly reached into my pocket for the whisperstone.

"Leona, are you there?"

"Yes, I'm here. Any trouble up there?"

"Maybe. There's someone coming toward us on the beach, but I'm not sure yet if she's a threat. I'm going to go talk with her."

In my mind's eye, I saw Leona frown. "You want me to shadow you?"

"That... might be a good idea. But I'm going now. Can't wait."

I pocketed the whisperstone and cast a quick warding spell as I ran down the back side of the rock and rounded the corner.

"Halt!" I called, slowing to a walk. "Who goes there?"

The woman froze, fear etched across her face. She took a stumbling step backward. "Please, don't hurt me. I've come alone."

"Who are you?" I asked again, still striding across the sand. "What's your name?"

She trembled and hugged her chest, in what appeared to be genuine fear. "My name is Aurora, and I've escaped from the cult led by Malachai." She hesitated for a moment. "Are you the Tidecaller?"

"You're alone?"

"Yes," she said quickly. "I promise, no one followed me."

I used my magic to test that, and as far as I could tell, there was no one else but her. Neither was she using a whisperstone or some other magical means to communicate with someone more distant.

"Why are you here?"

She took a deep breath. "Malachai has found the last piece of the Tidecaller's Amulet. I thought he would use it for good, but when we were chasing your ship into the whirlpool, he turned violent. I realized that everything he had told us was a lie. When we came out of the vortex, I saw my chance and jumped into the water. They probably think that I'm dead."

"Are they still hunting for us out there?"

"I don't know. Your magic is very good, which is why they haven't found you yet. They probably think you sailed to one of the other islands by now."

I smirked. "Probably. After all, we would be crazy to run our ship aground at low tide."

"Is... is that what actually happened?"

Leona chose that moment to appear, sword in hand. "Sam, who is this?"

"A friend, I think," I said quickly. "She says her name is Aurora, and she recently escaped from the cult. She has some information that may prove useful."

Leona's eyes narrowed. "You think we can trust her?"

"Yes," I told her, remembering my brief vision from the scrystone compass. Aurora's fear was no less palpable now than it had been then. I wanted to help her.

"Please," she said urgently. "I can help you get the amulet back. I know where he's going with it."

"And why would you help us?" Leona asked.

"Because I've seen what he plans to do with that power. He's a cruel and dangerous man. He won't ever stop hunting you as long as the amulet exists."

A chill ran down my back at her words. I knew she had spoken the truth.

"So where is he taking the amulet?" Leona asked. "And why would he leave this place, if he knows we're here?"

"Because he doesn't know you're here," Aurora answered. "He thinks that you escaped. But Malachai is a very patient man. He'll take the amulet back to his base in the Corsair Isles for safekeeping, and then—"

"Wait," I said. "Malachai has a base in the Corsair Isles?"

"Where?" Leona asked. "Which island?"

Aurora looked at each of us and blinked. "Do you have a map? Perhaps it would be best to show you."

Leona shot me a meaningful look. At length, she sighed.

"Very well. Come with me."

The tide had mostly come in by now, and the *Ebony Eagle* was standing mostly upright. Within an hour or two, we'd be free to set sail—provided, of course, that the cultists weren't lying in wait for us nearby.

"Do you trust me, Samuel?" Aurora asked softly as we waded out to the launch, her eyes searching my own.

"For now," I told her, feeling unsure.

She nodded. "I suppose that's the best I can expect. But please know that I want to redeem myself, in all of your eyes."

I wanted to believe her—and deep down, I suppose I did. For a moment, I considered telling her about the vision I'd had of her through the scrystone compass, but I decided against it. After all, I hadn't even shared that with Leona yet.

We took the oars and roared across the gentle waters of the lagoon to our waiting ship. After handing the launch off to the crew, who were already taking down our temporary camp on the beach, we climbed the rope ladder to the deck and proceeded to the captain's cabin.

"All right," said Leona, laying out her maps on the wooden table in the center of the room. "Show us the location of Malachai's base."

From her tone, I could tell she was still skeptical, but Aurora didn't seem to notice at all. Instead, she leaned forward and pored over the carefully detailed maps (which were quite impressive, especially considering the lawlessness of the territory they covered). Meanwhile, Leona's hand slipped quietly to the dagger partially hidden in her tunic. I knew that if Aurora tried anything, that dagger would end up in her back.

"There," she said, pointing to a long, narrow stretch of land on the outskirts of the archipelago. "Malachai's base is there."

Leona frowned, and her grip tightened on the hilt of her dagger. "There's nothing on that island, girl. It's little more than a sandbar with some trees."

"I know—that's why Malachai chose it. The base itself is underground."

Leona raised an eyebrow. "An underground base on a sandbar?"

"Yes. He uses dark sorcery to keep the water out. The entrance lies here," Aurora continued, pointing to the map again. "It's disguised by an old shipwreck."

Leona peered at the map for a few moments. To my relief, her grip on the hilt of her dagger loosened.

"Well, I'll be damned. There is a shipwreck on that point, if memory serves me right."

"You sail the Corsair Isles often?" Aurora asked innocently.

Leona laughed. "Often? It's practically my second home, honey. I'm a privateer."

"When should we leave?" I asked Aurora.

She paused. "Malachai might have left a longboat to watch for you, but with your magic, we should be able to give them the slip. Everyone else was going north."

Leona's expression hardened ever so slightly. I could tell that she still wasn't entirely convinced of Aurora's intentions. Before she could speak, I turned to her.

"In that case, Captain, I think we should set sail at once. I can maintain the concealing spell until we're safely away from the atoll."

"Very well," Leona said at length. "In that case, we sail within the hour."

We climbed to the top of the aftcastle and silently observed the men making their final preparations. As the seas finally reached high tide, the deck began to rock in the gentle waves. Leona gave her orders softly, maintaining the profound silence, and the men unfurled just one sail. Raising my hands, I called upon my magic to fill it and send us out.

Now we find out if Aurora is actually a traitor, I thought silently, exchanging a grim look with Leona. This time, her hand was on her sword hilt. If the cultists took us down, she would make damn sure that Aurora went down with us.

But Aurora seemed oblivious to all that. She leaned innocently over the railing, her eyes filled with childlike wonder as we pulled out of the gentle lagoon and unfurled the rest of our sails. As the dolphins began to dance off our bow, she stifled a cry of pure delight.

"We don't have to stay quiet now, you know," I told her.

"Oh, I know," she said, blushing a little. "It's just... I've never been on a ship without also pulling an oar."

Her words touched something in me, and I thought again of the girl from my vision, her life little more than different shades of fear. We kept a close watch on the horizon for the next few hours, but the seas were empty—no enemy in sight. And as we watched the gorgeous sunset off our port bow, I couldn't help but feel that it would be good to see her open up and blossom, now that she was truly free.

In Which I Learn the Terrible Truth About My Long-Lost Family

It felt good to stand atop the aftcastle of the *Ebony Eagle* again, gazing out across the waters as the wind whipped my shaggy hair. This was where I belonged—aboard a ship on the open ocean. We were leaving the Cerulean Sea behind us, sailing north for the Corsair Isles. The last time I'd sailed to that lawless archipelago, I'd barely escaped with my life. But that hardly mattered now.

"Samuel," said Leona, interrupting my idle musings. "We need to talk."

"What is it?" I asked.

She glanced pointedly at the bow, where Aurora stood gazing out across the ocean. Ever since we'd left the lagoon, she'd spent most of her time there, lost in thought.

"I don't trust her," said Leona, keeping her voice low. "How did she get past that whirlpool to find us? Are we sure she's not still working for Malachai?"

I frowned. "You think she's leading us into a trap?"

"Could be. I think you've got a blind spot for her, which would be the perfect opening for a skilled liar to manipulate you."

"We don't know that," I said, bristling at the implication. "Why would she betray us now?"

Leona shrugged, affecting an air of nonchalance. "It's not personal, Sam. I just can't shake the feeling that there's something she's not telling us."

"We can trust her," I insisted.

"Are you sure?"

"Of course," I said quickly. "Her best opportunity to betray us was back at the atoll, when we were most vulnerable to attack. Besides..." I hesitated, unsure whether to share the vision that I'd had with the scrystone compass. Would Leona accept that?

"I know you like her, Sam," Leona said carefully. "But before we get to the Corsair Isles, I need her to tell me everything she knows."

"All right. I'll go talk with her, if that's what you want."

I left Leona on the upper deck and approached Aurora at the bow of the ship. Her eyes were guarded as she turned to face me.

"Hey," I said, standing alongside her. "Got a moment to talk?"

"Of course," she said softly, her face still partially concealed by her hood. She stared demurely at the water below, where the dolphins were happily riding our wake.

"I don't mean to bother you," I said quickly. "It's just..."

"The captain doesn't trust me, does she?"

I sighed. "Not particularly, no. She wanted me to talk with you, but I would have come over whether or not she put me up to it."

To my surprise, she smiled. "Thanks, Samuel. I'm glad."

An awkward silence fell between us, though I suspect it was more awkward for me than for her. She was still surrounded by so much mystery that I hardly knew how to breach it.

"So tell me, how did you first pick up the magical arts?" I asked, grasping at something to talk about. "You don't strike me as a someone who went through formal mage training."

"No," she said, shaking her head. "One tends to learn things quickly when their survival depends on it."

"Your survival?"

"Growing up in Malachai's cult was... a very dangerous thing." She paused, looking up at me. "Another thing I picked up quickly was how to recognize a kindred spirit."

I frowned. What was she trying to say? Perhaps she was just lonely, having left the cult and all her former connections behind.

"I'm sure it was," I said uneasily. "You said you grew up in the cult. Did you ever know your family?"

"A little bit," she answered. "I can still remember my mother."

"I never knew my mother. I was raised by my father."

"And I never knew my father," she said softly. "But my mother used to sing me a lullaby about him. The feeling it gave me still haunts my dreams."

"I know what you mean," I said, realizing that I'd had much the same experience. It was one of those memories that you forget about, until something unexpectedly recalls it. Without thinking, I began to hum the lullaby my grandmother used to sing to me.

"That's it," said Aurora—though strangely, she did not seem surprised. As if to confirm, she began to hum it herself.

"You know it?" I asked, my eyes widening.

"Yes."

She glanced meaningfully at the scrimshaw locket hanging from my neck, the only memento I had from my long-lost mother. Her gaze lingered for a moment before she turned away.

"Aurora," I said, my mind suddenly racing. "Your mother... was she from these parts?"

"Yes, she was. Before she died, she tried to return home to the islands in the Cerulean Sea. She told me a lot about them."

"But your father—he was from the north, wasn't he?"

She drew a deep breath, turning her gaze back out to the ocean ahead of us. "Isn't it strange, how fate binds people together?"

"It is," I said, my heart now racing.

"We all have secrets," she mused, swaying gently with the ship as it rose and fell. "But sometimes, those secrets connect us to each other in unexpected ways."

My breath caught in my throat. I had a feeling I knew where she was going.

"Is there something you want to share with me, Aurora?"

She paused for a moment, then nodded. "It's not just our history with the cult that binds us, Samuel. You are my brother, and I am your sister."

"My... sister?" I asked, the words sounding impossible on my tongue. "How can that be?"

"Our parents were both caught up in the cult, but our father escaped, while our mother did not. That's how we became separated."

Her words struck me like a physical blow. The crashing of the waves against the hull of the ship seemed to echo the tempest that now threatened to rage within me. Memories began to flood back, each more painful than the last—but still, I had to know.

"Tell me everything," I demanded, leaning closer.

"Our parents joined the cult before we were born. They were genuine believers, until they discovered the truth about the dark powers that they served. Desperate to escape, they made plans to flee with both of us, but Malachai discovered their intentions."

"What happened then?" I asked.

She drew a long breath. "Malachai sees everyone as a pawn. He allowed father to escape, believing that he could better manipulate them if they were separated." She paused, biting her lip. "He wasn't wrong."

A sharp pang of grief and anger shot through me at the thought of our parents being torn apart from one another. I clenched my fists, holding onto the rail with whitened knuckles.

"Father never told me anything about being caught up in the cult."

"That's probably because you were too young to understand," she told me. "We both were, just in different ways. As for me, I was always so close to it that I didn't know any other way."

"Where's our mother? What happened to her?"

A mask of sadness suddenly fell over Aurora's face. "She's gone," she said, her words heavy with grief.

"Gone? How?"

"She died trying to escape," Aurora explained. "She tried to run away with me, back to the isles of her birth, but Malachai wouldn't let her take me. I don't know how it happened exactly, but she died in the struggle."

"But... why?" I stammered. "What did Malachai want you for?"

"The same reason he wants you," she said bitterly. "For our 'unique heritage.'"

"The Tidecaller's Amulet," I mused aloud. More than ever before, I wanted to see it destroyed.

Aurora nodded sadly. "Malachai had hoped that I would be able to wield it and groomed me for that very purpose. But when it became clear that I could not, he shifted his plans to you."

"He's been watching me from the shadows this entire time?"

She nodded. "Malachai is a very patient man. With the family support you grew up with, he knew he couldn't break you until you'd hit a low. That's why he waited until after your friend Jason was knighted, leaving you without a ship. He knew that you wouldn't move back in with your grandparents as a grown man, since that would be an admission of failure."

"But... why didn't our father ever tell me?"

"Probably to protect you. If you knew too much, there was a danger you'd seek out the cult on your own."

"Even after what they did to our mother?"

"I doubt that father ever knew what became of her. Bringing you up safely was more important than winning her back, and to do that, he had to stay as far from the cult as possible."

I drew a sharp breath. Things that I'd never thought to be connected were suddenly coming together in my mind. I realized that my father had been preparing me to resist the cult this whole time; that was why Malachai had resorted to force instead of persuasion to win me over. As for my mother, my father had always told me that I would find her someday. That was what the scrimshaw locket had been for. If he couldn't save her, he wanted me to save her instead.

My expression hardened. "We can't let their sacrifices be in vain."

"We can't," Aurora agreed.

"So what do we do now?"

She smiled and took my hand. "We sail for the Corsair Isles," she told me. "And when we get there, we do what we have to do to make sure that Malachai can never hurt us again."

* * *

For several days, I pondered Aurora's shocking revelation. Growing up without a mother, I knew that I was missing something in my life—but I'd never known that I had a sister, too. Why hadn't my father told me? Had he hoped to shield me from the cult? How in the seven seas was keeping a secret like that supposed to help me?

I'll spare you the long hours I spent wrestling with these questions, tossing and turning in my hammock. But as I awoke to another restless morning, I knew that I couldn't let the past consume me. I had to move forward—we both did, Aurora and me.

"Are you all right there, Sam?" Leona asked as I joined her at the helm. "You've been a little... subdued these last few days."

"It's Aurora," I admitted. "Ever since I learned that she's my sister, I haven't been able to stop thinking about it."

She nodded. "Sounds like the two of you need to have a good, long heart-to-heart. Only be careful, Sam. I'm still not sure we can trust her."

"What do you mean?" I asked, frowning. "She's my sister, my own flesh and blood."

"All the more reason to be cautious."

I stared at her, horrified. She caught my gaze and raised an eyebrow.

"I'm not saying you should reject her. Just remember: 'I against my brother; my brother and I against my cousin; my cousin, my brother, and I against the world.'"

"What in the blazes is that supposed to mean?"

"It means you should stop fuming and go talk with your sister. Don't let me come between the two of you."

I narrowed my eyes indignantly. "I think I will."

As usual, Aurora was perched at the top of the bow, admiring the view. Against the backdrop of the setting sun, dark tendrils of her long hair whipped around her face. My heart pounded a little faster as I walked up to her.

"Aurora?"

"Yes, Sam?"

"There's something I want to talk with you about."

"Sure. What would you like to know?"

I paused, considering my words. So many questions had occurred to me in the last few days, I hardly knew where to start.

"About our mother. You said that she died at Malachai's hands?"

"Yes," she said sadly. "I remember all too well."

"But if that's true, why did you stay? When she died, wouldn't that have shocked you so much that you would have found a way to leave the cult? Surely this isn't the first opportunity you've had to run away since then."

She drew a deep breath, as if recalling a painful memory. But when she turned to face me, something in her eyes was off somehow. I wasn't sure what it was, or even how I knew, really. But my arms tensed ever so slightly, and the hair on my neck began to bristle.

Stop that, Sam, I told myself. *She's your sister, for crying out loud!*

"Do you see those islands over there?" she asked, pointing to the horizon.

I squinted a little. "Yeah, that looks like the first of them."

"We're almost at Malachai's hideout. The Tide-caller's Amulet will be there, waiting for you."

"Of course."

"You are the only one who can wield it, you know."

I frowned. What was she talking about? I looked into her eyes and saw that they had glazed over, as if she had fallen into a trance. Her hand had slipped down to her belt. As I opened my mouth to speak, I caught a glint of steel. My eyes widened, but I was too slow.

In one smooth motion, she grabbed a tuft of my hair with her free hand and sliced upward with her blade. Immediately, I felt a sharp pain at the base of my skull. I screamed and fell to the deck, convulsing. Panicked, I reached inwardly to stem the outward flow of my powers, but they were slipping away like sand through a broken hourglass.

"No!" I cried out in desperation, grasping at the clumps of my hair that now littered the deck. But there was nothing I could do. My hair had been shorn, and with it, my magic.

I looked up just in time to meet Aurora's eyes before she leaped over the railing and dove into the water. In that moment, I saw the strangest mixture of grief and triumph, and probably a hundred other emotions besides. Then she disappeared over the edge, and I suddenly came back to my senses.

"Stop her!" I screamed. But she was already gone.

Shouts sounded all around me, and Leona quickly rushed to my side.

"What happened? Where's Aurora?"

"She—she cut my hair," I stammered.

Leona swore. "Find her!" she shouted to her men. "She can't have gone far!"

"But captain, she jumped over the edge."

"Aye—look! There she goes!"

Aurora appeared for only a moment, swimming swiftly away toward land. Too late, the archers nocked their bows. Perhaps it was only an illusion, but she vanished from view like a mermaid beneath the waves.

Leona clenched her fist and swore again, even more explicitly this time. Then, she turned to me.

"How bad is it, Sam? Did she hurt you? Are you bleeding?"

I rose unsteadily to my feet. As I did, the wind picked up, threatening to blow away my hair. Frantic not to lose it, I dropped to my knees and grabbed as much of it as I could.

"Save it!" I said, grasping at the stray strands. The other men helped me, and soon we had gathered it all up.

But it was no use. Shorn as it was, I could no more call on my magic through it than I could squeeze water from a stone. I was powerless—utterly powerless.

"It's all right, Sam," Leona told me. "We'll think of something."

"But Leona," I choked out, the enormity of it all crashing down on me. "We can't face the cultists—

not like this. Without my powers, there's no way we can win."

"Will they come back?" Leona asked.

I frowned. "What do you mean?"

"Your powers. Will they come back to you as your hair grows?"

"Yes, but—"

"Then we haven't lost yet," she said, looking me squarely in the eye. "You're alive, you're whole, and aside from the temporary loss of your powers, you're still in good shape. I know these isles like the back of my hand. All we've got to do is lay low for a while. No big deal."

But it was a big deal, and not just because of my hair. Aurora—*my sister*—how could she have betrayed me like this? It felt as if my whole world was crumbling, and not just from the loss of my hair. And though Leona tried to brush it off, I knew that we were in terrible danger. Malachai would stop at nothing to find us, and now that he knew we'd reached the Corsair Isles, all he had to do was blockade the archipelago until he found us. It was too late to turn back.

In Which I Feel Like Half a Man As We Scramble To Evade Our Enemies

The deck of the *Ebony Eagle* made a wide corkscrewing motion over the surging waves, the wind blowing nearly perpendicular to our course. As sailors, we were used to this, but I still clenched the railing of the upper deck uneasily. With my magic, I could have easily redirected the wind to blow on a more direct course, easing our passage. Unfortunately, the loss of my hair had also shorn me of my powers.

"Steady now," Leona murmured, her braided hair waving in the wind. "Keep her trimmed, lads." She fixed her steely gaze on the islands ahead of us, part of the lawless archipelago known as the Corsair Isles. Though she knew these parts well, without a sea mage we were as helpless as a motherless fawn before a pack of wolves.

"Do you think they know where we are?" I asked.

"I doubt it," Leona answered with a shrug. "Even if they had set someone to follow us, I think we lost them when we rounded that reef back there. Lots of pirate ships pass through these waters, and they won't want to get too close to any of them if they can help it."

"Yes, but if they do—"

"Relax, Sam. I know plenty of places where we can lie low. These isles are like a second home to me, after all. We'll wait until your hair grows back, then resume our mission as if nothing had happened. Malachai can't use the amulet without you, remember?"

I nodded, though I did not feel nearly as confident as she did. After all, it wasn't like my hair had been cut by accident. Aurora, my own sister—I still could hardly believe that she had betrayed me. Had the cult sucked her in so completely that she would turn on her own flesh and blood?

"I hope you don't plan to take us to Cole's Cove," I muttered. "My last trip there didn't end too well."

"Of course not," Leona replied with a chuckle. "Cole's Cove ain't exactly what I'd call 'lying low.' There are plenty of other places we can flee, though, and the pirates in these parts know me well enough to stay away. After all, there's a code—"

"The cultists don't follow a code, Leona," I interrupted. "And for all we know, they've infiltrated every pirate crew in these waters. Now that they have the amulet, all they need is to find and kidnap me."

Leona scoffed. "They'll need to do a lot more than kidnap you, Sam. I don't think you're the kind to break under pressure."

Was that true, though? I drew a deep breath, trembling a little in spite of myself. Malachai had such a hold over my sister that I hadn't been able to detect even a hint of her deception until it had been too late. And Soren—everything had been going in that man's favor, and yet he'd still given himself over to the cult. If Malachai was so charismatic that he could sway both of them to his power, how long would I last before his brainwashing finally broke me?

Sensing my thoughts, Leona put a hand on my arm. "Go down below, Sam. You should get some rest."

I nodded, offering no protest. After all, what use was I above deck?

"Your powers will come back soon enough," she reassured me. "Besides, you are more than just your magic. Remember that."

"Thanks," I muttered, turning to go.

Inside my cabin, I lay back in my hammock, staring at the ceiling as the ship dipped and swayed. My scalp itched almost constantly, leaking magical energy like a bucket riddled with holes. With nothing else to do, my mind turned again to Aurora. If it had been anyone else who had shorn me, I would have been able to put it out of my mind long enough to rest. But to know that my long-lost sister had deceived me... It was enough to make me question everything I thought I knew.

After a while, these thoughts were too much for me. I rose from the hammock and began to pace restlessly across the floor.

Surely there was something I could do about the loss of my powers. Yes, they would gradually return as my hair grew back, but I couldn't afford to wait that long—not with everyone depending on me. So, I opened the small chest where I'd placed what little of my hair I'd managed to recover. Something in the back of my mind had told me that I needed to save it, though what good it would do me, I did not know.

I closed my eyes as I clutched the lock of my hair in both hands. There was some degree of power there, but it was fading quickly, like flowers dying long after they have been cut. I tried to tap into it, to draw from it the way that I normally did, but it was like trying to suck water out of a stone.

"No good," I muttered, returning it to the chest. I was about to close it up again, when I remembered how Soren had stolen the amulet because I hadn't been wise enough to keep it with me. Was I missing something? Was I about to make some other mistake again?

I know it isn't exactly rational, but at that moment, I was loath to discard that lock of hair completely. Perhaps I couldn't bear the loss, but either way, I found myself looking for some way that I could carry that lock of hair with me. I don't exactly know why, but in my frazzled state of mind, I somehow felt that this was of critical importance.

I settled on my mother's scrimshaw locket, which I kept under my shirt at all times. There was just enough space inside of it to hold a lock of hair. Grunting a little as I shoved it in with both thumbs, I barely managed to close the locket again, but the hook finally swung over, securing it shut. And as I held it in my hands, I could feel the residual energy in my hair mingling with the familiar weight of the carved ivory.

"Cold comfort is better than none," I told myself, not really believing it. Still, it was better to hold onto it for now, even if it was also a reminder of my sister's awful betrayal.

I paced back and forth in the cramped confines of my cabin as I pondered over the leather-bound manuals of magic that I'd borrowed from Leona's quarters. They were far from comprehensive, possessing only a smattering of discussions on a random sampling of subjects, but I searched them anyway, desperate for some way to grow my hair.

After hours of searching, I'd stumbled upon a potion recipe that might do the trick. It was for reversing natural hair loss, but it was the closest thing I'd found so far. I traced my fingertips over the creased and age-worn page, mentally running through the list of ingredients. Some of them, like powdered dragon scales, would be impossible to find, but perhaps I could find an adequate substitute from our stores.

It took me most of the day, but I managed to assemble the ingredients, finding substitutes for about half of them. All I could do was hope that those were sufficient, since I wasn't all that well versed in the art of brewing potions. But from how the concoction hissed and bubbled in the cauldron, I began to feel hopeful that this could really work.

At long last, I held a vial of thick pink liquid in front of me. It smelled absolutely vile, but I did my best to ignore that as I plugged my nose with my other hand.

“Here goes nothing,” I said, closing my eyes. Then, before I could rethink my decision, I chugged the whole thing down.

I ran to the mirror, hoping to watch as the potion took effect. But though I felt a slight tingling in my scalp, it was so faint that it could have just been my imagination. In the meantime, my stomach began growling in protest, threatening to evacuate itself explosively on the mirror. I held it in for as long as I could manage, then flung open the porthole window and retched over the side.

“Something tells me that’s not from seasickness,” Leona’s voice came from behind me. She held the empty vial at arm’s length, as if it were a piece of rotten fruit. It certainly smelled like one.

“Hello, Leona,” I groaned. My stomach still felt weak, so I lay back on my hammock, resting as best as I could.

“The quartermaster told me that you’d asked for some pretty strange stuff.” She nodded toward the cauldron. “You’re not going to blow up my ship, are you?”

“No. Just trying to regrow my hair.”

“Give it a rest, Sam. Losing your mind over this isn’t going to make your hair grow back any faster.”

“Neither will doing nothing,” I snapped. “I hate this, Leona. I’m helpless without my magic.”

She sighed and flipped through the pages of the book on the table. “At least these old tomes are finally getting some use. I always wondered why I kept them around. Oh, look, a guide for growing nutritious sea kelp. Think that would work on your hair?”

The thought of eating kelp made my stomach go weak again. I barely made it to the porthole in time to empty its contents into the water.

Leona laughed as she excused herself. "Don't be too hard on yourself. Things will work themselves out."

Alone in my quarters again, I stumbled to my makeshift workbench and wearily sat on the stool. So much for potion making. My eyes fell again on the crudely cut lock of my hair, and I stuffed it back into the locket, wanting to never see it again. Imagine staring at your recently amputated limb, still spurting blood as the surgeon applies his tourniquet, and you'll have some idea of the revulsion I felt in that moment.

But then, my fingers fell on the compass that still hung around my neck. I pulled it out and examined it, wondering if perhaps the scrystone could be of some help. It had been several days since Aurora's betrayal, and in that time, a very small portion of my magic had come back. So as I stared into the scrystone, I was surprised but not shocked to feel my scalp start to tingle.

I took a deep breath and channeled as much magic as I could muster into the smooth, glassy stone. As I did so, images began to parade across the back of my mind, fuzzy and indistinct. I thought I saw an altar, adorned with blood-red candles and other items of dark magic. And there, resting atop it, was the Tidecaller's Amulet, now fully assembled and pulsing with untapped energy.

I groaned. "Yes, I know that Malachai possesses the reconstructed amulet. Show me something *useful,* please."

The image shifted, and I saw the amulet in my hands. I tried in vain to crush it, summoning all manner of spells. Nothing worked until I plucked a strand of my hair and laid it across the amulet. It instantly crumbled into powder, its magic dissipating. But so did all of my hair—and with it, my powers.

I opened my eyes and gasped. With awful clarity, I suddenly understood that the only way to destroy the Tidecaller's Amulet was to permanently lose my magic. I would have to find some way to live with that, not just for a season, but for the rest of my life.

Was that really worth it? Or was I making a terrible mistake?

With a heavy heart, I stepped out of the cabin and climbed the stairs to the upper deck of the *Ebony Eagle.* Leona stood behind the helm, warily watching the waters around us.

"Afternoon, Sam," she greeted me. "Any luck getting your hair to grow?"

"None," I said, leaning against the railing. We were sailing between some rocks, the wild shores of a large untamed island passing off to our starboard side. Leona steered us deftly, hugging the coastline to keep us hidden from view.

"It's only a matter of time," she said, trying to reassure me. But her words offered little comfort.

"Leona," I told her, fingering the scrystone compass. "Even after my hair does grow back, I don't know how much help I'm going to be."

She sighed. "Now, Sam—"

"No really, this is something you need to hear. There are consequences for destroying the amulet. As part of the process, I may lose my powers forever."

My words made her frown. "What are you saying, Sam?"

"You know how I'm the only person who can wield the amulet? It turns out that destroying the amulet may destroy my powers as well."

"We don't know that for sure."

"No," I admitted, "but while studying ways to grow out my hair again, I saw a vision of what it will take to destroy the Tidecaller's Amulet. There will be consequences."

Leona took a few moments to consider my words, then shrugged. "We'll deal with that when the time comes. Until then, let's just focus on staying alive."

"But—"

"If you want to make yourself useful in the meantime, try to find out if there's some other way. For now, though, survival is our first priority."

As if in answer, the lookout on the crow's nest sounded the alarm. "Enemy ship!" he shouted. "We've been spotted!"

Leona and I frowned and peered at the waters off our port side. Sure enough, a longboat was rounding the headland, turning to bear down on us. At the bow stood a bald-headed sorcerer, the telltale glow of magic emanating from his hands.

"Evasive maneuvers!" Leona shouted as a ball of crackling energy hurtled toward us.

I braced myself as it struck us. Our magical wards held for the most part, but the energy still washed over the deck, bringing several of us to our knees. It was a binding spell of some kind, an attempt to immobilize us and leave us adrift as easy pickings for a boarding party. But thankfully, the wards still held.

"Sam!" Leona yelled. My heart sank as I realized she was asking me for help that I could not give. I lifted my hands anyway, trying to summon what power I could, but all my efforts felt like pushing on a string.

Another blast of energy struck our ship—this time, in the form of a fireball. Flames erupted across the deck, threatening to turn the *Ebony Eagle* into an inferno.

"Man the pumps!" Leona shouted. "Get the hose on deck!"

The crew worked quickly, but without my magic to enhance them, their efforts were sluggish and weak. They managed to put out most of the fires before the wood took to the magical flames, but not without a few of them getting dangerously singed.

By now, we were at full sail. The next few moments were critical. If my windcasting powers hadn't been handicapped, we could have pulled ahead, putting crucial distance between us and our pursuers as Leona sought refuge among the rocks. Instead, we had to use what crosswinds nature provided for us, making our sailing much less efficient. I clenched my fists as I watched the cultists creep ever closer.

"Starboard!" Leona's voice cut through the cacophony on deck. She turned the helm hard, just as a flight of arrows fell to the water on our other side.

Panic clawed at my chest—we were under fire, and there was nothing—literally nothing—that I could do.

"Watch out!" I yelled as the cultists opened fire again—this time, with flaming fire arrows. Unlike the magical flames, those would catch easily on both wood and sail.

Without warning, Leona turned hard to port, letting the crosswinds carry us. The ship tilted dangerously, nearly throwing me off my feet, but we evaded the worst of the volley. Our top mainsail took to the flames, though, and the winds spread it dangerously fast, threatening to bring down the others.

In desperation, I tried again to draw on my magic. If only I could summon a small waterspout, that would easily douse the flames. And now was the critical moment. If we lost the topsail, the cultists would surely overtake us.

A tingling sensation spread across my scalp. I closed my eyes and drew even deeper, until the tingling turned to a burning pain. It felt as if my hair were being ripped out by the roots, but still I pressed on, heedless of the chaos and cacophony all around me. Like a frantic climber scrambling at a sheer rocky face for the barest purchase, I pulled on my fragile magic until my body shook and my legs threatened to give out beneath me.

"Look out!" someone shouted.

The waterspout was pathetic by my usual standards—little more than a whale's spray, really—but it got the job done. The flames quickly died, leaving the singed topsail flapping uselessly in the wind, but men were already scrambling up the rigging and across the yard to secure it again.

The deck seemed to spin beneath me, and I fell like a limp marionette whose strings have been cut. My strength was so totally exhausted that I couldn't even keep my head from bouncing like a dropped melon when it hit the deck.

"Sam!"

Leona's voice was the last I heard before I passed out.

In Which We Go From Being Stranded in the Corsair Isles to Something Much Worse

When I came to, I found myself lying on the deck of the *Ebony Eagle.* The blazing sun beat down relentlessly, casting harsh shadows and causing my sweat to bead. I groaned and sat up, noticing the conspicuous lack of shade. Our once-proud mast lay broken and splintered, the yard and mainsail draped uselessly over the edge of our battered ship. Without it, we were drifting at the mercy of the sea.

I looked around quickly, expecting to see the cultists bearing down on us, but their longboats were nowhere in sight. Somehow, Leona had managed to escape them.

"Salvage everything you can!" Leona shouted. I rose to my feet and walked over to her side.

"What happened?"

"You missed the worst of it," she told me. "We got away, but just barely. Had to rig up a makeshift sail with the jibs—ugliest thing I've ever seen."

She scowled as she pointed toward the bow, where her men had managed to drape a torn sail across the bowsprit. It was barely functional, unable to turn us either right or left. For Leona to see her fast, sleek ship shattered and broken like this had to be at least as bad as losing my hair had been for me.

"We'll fix her up, Captain," I tried to reassure her. "The *Ebony Eagle* will sail again."

"Not unless we get out of here," she muttered. "There's no wood suitable for building masts in these parts. We'll have to leave her in that cove and hope for the best."

I bit my lip and nodded. Neither of us wanted to say it aloud, but I could tell that we both knew it wouldn't take long for the cultists to find us without a proper concealing spell. "I'll get to work with the others," I told her. She nodded curtly, and I turned to join the rest of the crew.

We quickly loaded the launch with all the food, water, and other supplies it would hold. The faces of the crew were grim and exhausted, and I could feel the weight of uncertainty as we prepared to go ashore.

"We'll ground the *Eagle* on the sands of that cove," Leona told me. "No sense in scuttling her when all she needs is a new mast. We have enough supplies to last two weeks, if we ration them carefully."

"What about after that?" I asked.

She pursed her lips, her eyes narrowing. "If the cultists haven't gotten us by then, we'll take the launch and hope enough of your powers have come back to see this thing to the end."

"And if not?"

She didn't answer.

We landed and hauled the *Eagle* as high up on the beach as we could. She listed slightly as she came to rest, and we unloaded the rest of the supplies directly. I was nervous at first that she'd be too visible, but without her mast, the only way to see her was to sail by the mouth of the cove.

Leona sent out some scouts while the rest of the crew set up camp. We worked quickly, every man knowing his role. Our long-term plans were still up in the air, but there was enough to occupy our immediate attention that we didn't need to think about that. By the time the sun hung low on the horizon, the scouts had all returned, confirming that our little islet was indeed empty. For the moment, we were secure.

"How are you holding up, Sam?" Leona asked after hearing their report. "Anything new with your magic?"

I shook my head, unable to hide my frustration. "It's still too weak. I can feel it growing, but there's just not enough to tap into it fully." I paused for a moment, staring into the dancing flames of the cooking fire. "Sorry, Leona. I'm useless without my magic."

"That's not true," Leona said firmly. "You are more than just your magic."

"Yeah, but what you need right now is a proper sea mage, not just another disheveled, shaggy-haired sailor."

She paused, considering her words. "I'm not going to lie, Sam. A lot of things would be easier for us if you still had your powers. But I know how to improvise when things go awry. This isn't the worst fix we've found ourselves in—not even close. And I would much rather have a sharp-minded sea mage who's temporarily lost his powers than a dull-minded one with all the magic in the world and no idea how to use it. Understand?"

"Yeah," I said at length. "Thanks."

She grinned and slapped me on the back. "We'll have you ship-shape in no time, Sam. It's only a matter of time and cosmetology. And when you are, those yellow-bellied cultists will be sorry that the only thing they took was your hair."

And not even that, I thought, fingering the locket under my shirt.

At that moment, a cry from the lookout echoed through the air. The men all leaped to their feet, grabbing their swords and bows. My only weapon was a dagger, so I peered out toward the mouth of the cove, my heart racing.

"Ship ahoy!" the lookout shouted again.

"Stow it!" Leona snapped. "We don't want to give ourselves away."

But it appeared that whoever was aboard the approaching ship already seen us, considering how they'd turned to head straight for the cove. My only consolation was that the ship was a square-rigged caravel, much like the *Eagle,* instead of one of the cultists' longboats. Still, given that these were the Corsair Isles, we were anything but safe.

"Are they friend or foe?" I asked uncertainly.

Leona peered at them, ignoring my question. Then suddenly, she cursed and spat.

"I should have known that sea witch would be the one to find me."

"That's Isadora?" I asked.

"Aye. That's her, all right. Of all the cursed luck."

"Maybe she's come in peace," I said, trying to sound optimistic.

But from the grim look on Leona's proud face, it was clear she didn't believe it for an instant.

We all watched silently as the launch approached the shore, Isadora standing at the prow. She cut a striking figure, with her piercing eyes and her blond, shimmering hair. As her men hauled the launch onto the beach, she leaped onto the sand. They flanked her on either side as she approached us.

"Leona," she said, nodding a curt greeting. "Samuel."

"Isadora," said Leona, sneering petulantly as she folded her arms. Isadora did the same.

"It seems that we find ourselves at an impasse," Isadora began. "Both of us want the amulet, which is now in Malachai's hands."

"Speak plainly," Leona snapped. "Do you mean to suggest an alliance?"

Isadora nodded. "Neither of us wanted it to come to this, but Malachai is a threat to all of us. He must be stopped. We both know that we stand a better chance of defeating him if we work together."

"And what happens after we win?" I asked. "Who gets the amulet then?"

"No one," she said, looking me in the eye. "My objective is to destroy it. Or barring that, to throw it into the deepest sea trench I can find."

I blinked in surprise. All this time, I'd assumed that Isadora was only interested in selling the amulet to the highest bidder, like the pirate she was. But if she truly wanted to destroy it, that changed everything.

Before I could point this out, though, Leona was already sniping back at her.

"We don't need your help," she scoffed. "We're doing just fine on our own."

"Are you kidding?" said Isadora, gesturing to the crippled *Ebony Eagle.* "Your ship is beached and out of commission. Where are you—"

"We've had a few minor setbacks, true, but they haven't put us out of action. Malachai's hideout is only a league or two away, and with Sam's magic I'm confident we can get that amulet back on our own."

I frowned. "Uh, Leona..."

"You're crazy," said Isadora, clenching her fists in frustration. "Can't you see that this is too important to squabble over pride? Malachai has to be stopped before he unlocks the power of that amulet. Everything depends on it."

Leona spat angrily onto the ground. "Which is why I absolutely refuse to work with you. How do I know you won't betray us at the critical moment? Just like you did before."

Isadora bit her lip, obviously wounded by Leona's remark. But the fact that she didn't try to hide it seemed to go right over Leona's head.

"I know I betrayed you in the past," Isadora said softly. "Is there no way I can make it right?"

"You can start by leaving us the hell alone!" Leona snapped. "Come on, Sam. We've got more important things to do than listen to this plotting sea witch."

"Wait, Leona," I protested. "I think we should listen to—"

"I said, let's go!"

Isadora took a deep breath and drew herself up. "I'll give you until morning. Hopefully that will give you enough time to quench your passions and see reason. Until then."

With that, she turned back to the launch, her men falling in step behind her. Leona scowled as we watched them go.

"I hate how she always has to get the last word."

I stared at her. "Did you not hear a single thing that she said?"

"Oh, I heard enough. And I'll be damned before I fight alongside her again."

"Will you damn the rest of us, too? We need her help, Leona—we can't defeat Malachai on our own."

"Give it time," she told me. "Your powers are already starting to return. Besides, we've broken into harder strongholds than this one."

I opened my mouth to protest, but she turned on her heel and headed back to the camp. Standing on the beach between the two rival captains, it felt like Leona was turning her back on me as, well. For a moment, I wondered if perhaps I shouldn't try to reach out to Isadora on my own. But Leona would rightfully see that as a betrayal and never forgive me for it.

As I turned to follow Leona back to the camp, I was overtaken by a sense of foreboding. How long would it take for the cultists to find us? Unless I could find some way to change Leona's mind, I feared that every delay was a potentially fatal mistake.

Dawn's light did little to dispel the tension of the previous night. A prickling sensation spread across my scalp, running down to the base of my spine. I nervously twirled a lock of hair between my fingers.

"Something's wrong," I told Leona. She looked at me and frowned.

"What are you talking about, Sam?"

"We should have given Isadora our answer last night, instead of waiting until dawn. We gain nothing by drawing things out."

"And we gain nothing by jumping into that traitor's arms!" Leona snapped.

I knew I shouldn't push her, but I was just too tired to care.

"You're wrong," I said, ignoring the way she bristled at me. "If we'd jumped at her offer, we would have been free of this place by nightfall. Now, the cultists are coming, and there's little we can do."

"Then let them come!" she roared.

Have you ever heard the expression "speak of the devil, and he will appear"? There's a lot of truth in that. One of the things that non-gifted people don't realize is that words have a magic of their own.

The invitation had barely escaped Leona's lips before the cultists were upon us. They emerged from the shadowy jungle without warning, brandishing rune-etched staves. Moving in eerie silence, they rushed our camp on the beach, swarming us like flies to a rotting carcass.

"To me!" Leona shouted, drawing her sword. But it was too late. The camp had been thrown into chaos, with every man struggling on his own as best he could.

Caught unawares, we were totally outmatched. A few men were able to draw their swords before the enemy fell upon us, but most of us had to use whatever we could grab. One man wielded a cast-iron pot from the fire, flinging its contents into the hooded eyes of the nearest attacker, who howled in pain. Others rushed forward, though, their staves raining down blows and beating us to the earth.

We fell back to the beach in a fighting retreat. But as the waves lapped our feet, it became clear that we were trapped.

"Stay behind me, Sam!" Leona shouted as she fought off an attacker. Though her opponent was larger and stronger than her, she dispatched him with a swift riposte to the throat. He fell into the surf with blood spurting from his neck.

I lifted my hands and called upon my magic, trying to summon fiery hailstones from the sky. But instead of flames, harmless ashes drifted down on us, and the effort to cast even that much of a spell left me utterly exhausted.

Then, just at our moment of greatest need, I turned and saw a boat rowing toward us across the waters.

"It's Isadora!"

Leona turned just in time to see her rival join the fray. The blond-haired pirate captain leaped from the boat, sword in one hand and crossbow in the other. She loosed a bolt into the hooded face of the nearest cultist, then plunged headlong into the melee, her blade flashing as she rallied her men.

"This way, boys! Show them what we're made of!"

A parade of mixed emotions ran across Leona's face. She settled on grim determination, pushing ahead without waiting for Isadora to join her.

That proved to be a mistake.

Two of the cultists cut her off, leaving her isolated and surrounded. Her blade flashed, but one of them struck her hand, disarming her, while another rushed forward with a large sack. Our eyes met for a brief moment, but in the next, they had the bag over her head.

"Leona!" I shouted. But it was too late. The cultists had her.

I turned and saw Isadora's men begin to fall as well. Perhaps if our forces had been combined from the outset, we could have fought off the cultists' ambush. But there had simply been too many of them.

I tried to summon my magic again, but before I could make any headway, I felt a binding spell come upon me again. I struggled in vain against it as a hooded figure rushed forward with another sack. Disarmed and powerless, there was nothing I could do but fall to the ground as they took me captive.

In Which We Come To Some Important Realizations While In Captivity

The cold, unyielding stone floor of our prison cell sapped the warmth from my body. I shivered, the salty dampness clinging to my skin. I was still wearing the same clothes from when they'd taken me, though my other belongings were gone. The rough-hewn walls glistened with moisture, trickling down to form small pools on the uneven floor. Our only source of light was a grimy lantern hanging just outside the door to our cell. Its eerie, flickering glow danced across Isadora's stoic features and Leona's bitter scowl.

"Feels like the sea itself is closing in on us," I murmured, my voice a hoarse whisper.

"Aye," Isadora agreed. "This place... it saps the hope right outta you."

A rat scurried along the edge of the room, pausing just a moment to regard me with its beady eyes. Before I could react, it scampered into a crack in the wall.

"How are your powers, Sam?" Leona asked, leaning in close to keep anyone outside from overhearing. "Now would be a great time for your sorcery."

I ran my fingers through my hair, feeling the faintest thrum of magic pulse through my tangled locks. It was a mere fraction of my previous powers, nowhere near enough to break us free.

"Sorry," I murmured. "We're going to have to find another way out of here."

Footsteps sounded in the hall outside, cutting our conversation short. A key clicked in the lock, and the door creaked open, revealing Malachai himself, flanked by cloaked guards on either side.

"Samuel," he said, his sibilant voice filling the room with eerie charisma. "It is time to embrace your destiny."

The Tidecaller's Amulet hung from his neck, complete and reassembled. My eyes widened as they fell upon it. The fragments fit together so perfectly, it was as if it had never been fractured—or perhaps that was an effect of the powerful magic that now emanated from it. I could feel its ominous pulse beckoning to me, tempting me to call upon its power.

Malachai grinned wickedly. "You want this, don't you?"

"No," I answered, a little too quickly.

"Here," he said, holding it out to me. "Join us, Samuel. Embrace your true power, as you were always meant to. It is your destiny."

I swallowed, my heart hammering in my chest. His words were honeyed poison, tempting me with promises of strength and control. But deep down, I knew that his offer did not come without a price. I took a deep breath and met his steady gaze.

"Go to hell, Malachai. I refuse to play any part in your plans."

His grin faltered and fell, his eyes cold and unforgiving. "So be it," he said icily. "If you refuse to join us willingly, then perhaps we can find... other means of persuasion."

I was prepared to endure torture. Everyone has their breaking point, of course, and mine is probably not much higher than average. But I had already resolved to endure as much of it as I could—and more importantly, I was expecting it. But when his cold, beady eyes fell on Leona, my stomach fell through the floor.

"Forget about me, Sam!" she snapped. "Let this creep do his worst. I've endured more pain than his thugs can inflict upon me."

"I doubt that very much," said Malachai, his evil grin returning.

"Don't worry, Leona," I said, clenching my fists. "I won't break so easily."

"That's the spirit, lad," said Isadora. Then, to Malachai, "Is that all you've got?"

"Such loyalty," he remarked, almost off-handedly. "But your devotion to one other is ultimately useless. In the end, every knee will bow to our cause."

I drew myself up, expecting the argument to turn into a full-blown confrontation. But Malachai casually turned and walked away, leaving the guards to close the door behind him. There was no sense of urgency to his retreat, nor even a sense that he was retreating at all. Instead, it seemed that he'd merely lost interest—that he had all the time and power in the world to bend us to his will.

The door slammed shut with a deafening finality, plunging us into darkness once more. I slumped against the wall and let out a breath I didn't know I'd been holding.

"Well, that was just dandy," Leona muttered. "So kind of him to welcome us to this place."

"Oh, stow it, Leona," Isadora answered, her voice piercing the eerie silence like a double-edged blade. "We wouldn't be here now if not for your foolish pride."

"Oh, that's rich," Leona retorted. "For all we know, you led them right to us."

In the dim light of our cell, Isadora's lips pulled back in a snarl. "Just what are you accusing me of?"

"I think you've been in league with that eel since the beginning."

I groaned and buried my head in my arms, my back pressed against the rough-hewn stone as I wondered if it would have been better to endure Malachai's torture.

"Oh, please," Isadora fired back, her words dripping with contempt. "Don't pretend to be some noble martyr after all the double-crosses you've pulled."

"Double-crossing? You want to talk about double-crossing? You who started this feud in the first place!"

"Excuse me?"

"You heard me!" Leona shouted, bristling as her eyes flashed dangerously. "We were blood sisters once, Isadora. But then—"

"That's enough!" I bellowed, silencing them both. "I have had it up to here with both of you! This is no time for petty squabbles!"

"Sam's right," Leona said quickly. "Now cool it, Isadora, and don't get in our way. I promise we won't leave you—"

"I said stop it, Leona!" I snapped. "This bickering is getting us nowhere!"

Leona's eyes narrowed. "You seriously think we can trust her?"

"Maybe," I said, turning to Isadora. "I'd at least like to hear her side of things."

Isadora laughed bitterly. "You really think I'm in league with Malachai? That I'm the reason we got caught up in this mess? Well, let me make one thing absolutely bloody clear: None of you hates Malachai more than I do. *None* of you."

"Why is that?" I asked, frowning.

"Because none of you fine folk were caught up in his cult. Like I was."

"You were?" Leona asked, her voice laced with suspicion.

Isadora took a deep breath. "Yes. I was seduced by his false promises and followed him blindly for years. It wasn't until much later that I saw the light and realized what I had become."

I glanced at Leona, wearily expecting to see a gloating look of triumph cross her face. To my surprise, she frowned in a look of genuine concern.

"How long ago was this, Isadora?" she asked.

Isadora bit her lip. "About the same time I betrayed you. And yes, I admit it—I betrayed you, Leona. Malachai pushed me to it. Are you happy now?"

"No," Leona answered quietly. "Isadora—I had no idea."

"Well, now you do," said Isadora, her shoulders tense as she fidgeted with her hands. After a moment's hesitation, she took a deep breath and glanced away. "I'm not proud of what I did—of what I became. You have every right to hate me. I just... I thought that if I could find the amulet before Malachai got his hands on it, I could at least make that much right."

I looked toward Leona, unsure of what to say. The captain's expression had softened considerably, and I could sense that the onetime rivals were sharing a significant moment.

"You're not a part of the cult anymore?" Leona asked.

"Hell, no!" Isadora answered emphatically. "I left them years ago, and I have spent all that time trying to put it behind me."

"Didn't Malachai try to hunt you down and force you back in?"

"He sure did," said Isadora, the fire returning to her eyes. "But I was stronger than he figured."

"You always were a bull-headed one," Leona muttered, though not unkindly. I could practically see the wheels turning in her mind as she weighed Isadora's words.

"I don't blame you for hating me, Leona," said Isadora. "Especially after how I treated you. I know I'd feel the same. But Malachai's plans are bigger than the two of us. We need to work together if we're going to defeat him. After that, you never have to see me again."

"Don't be a fool," said Leona, the barest hint of a grin on her face. "We all make mistakes. Not always as big as yours, but you never were one to go small."

Isadora raised an eyebrow. "Then you're saying our paths align?"

"More than that," said Leona, extending her hand. "I've seen the light, sister. Our rivalry ends here. I hope you can forgive me for treating you so harshly."

I let myself breathe again as the two captains embraced. And though they did their best to hide it, I could see that they both had tears in their eyes.

"Thank you, sister," Isadora said softly. "I couldn't ask for more."

"You're damn right," Leona said with a laugh. "Now, let's see if we can't find some way to break out of this waterlogged rat-hole. I've had enough of Malachai's hospitality to last a lifetime."

"Indeed," Isadora answered with a grin. "I couldn't have said it better myself."

A glimmer of light from the corridor danced on the rough stone walls of our cell, chasing away a bit of the darkness. I stirred from the corner, prepared to wake Leona and Isadora, but they were already alert.

"Who is it?" Isadora whispered as footsteps sounded in the hall.

"One man," Leona muttered, crouching catlike by the door. "Sam?"

I reached out with my magic, straining to draw as much power from my locks as I could. Thankfully, they had regrown just enough to grant me a sufficient measure of discernment. My magical senses confirmed what Leona said. I sensed a single guard in the hallway—and what was that?

"Hold on," I whispered, motioning for her to stand down. "Don't try to fight this one."

"Why not?" Isadora whispered frantically. The guard had almost reached our cell.

"His heart is filled with doubts. We may yet win him over."

Leona straightened at once, pulling a strand of hair behind her ear even though the guard couldn't yet see her. His footsteps stopped, and the food slot slid open.

"Good evening, sir," Leona said, her voice dripping honey as the guard slid us a tray of moldy bread and water. "I see our host's generosity knows no bounds."

"No need for sarcasm," the guard muttered reluctantly. Through the narrow window grill, I recognized him as one of the ones who had stood with Malachai earlier.

"My apologies," Leona answered meekly. "I meant no offense."

He grunted. "None taken, I suppose."

"Tell me, lad: What is your name?"

The guard hesitated, and for a heart-stopping moment, I feared he would simply walk away. But then, he answered.

"Gareth."

"Gareth," said Leona, giving me a grin. "That's a fine name. Why, one of the men on my crew carries that name."

"Aye. He's being held with the others in the dungeon below. The Master hasn't hurt him."

Though he left the word unspoken, it hung heavy in the air between us all: *The Master hasn't hurt him—yet.*

"I'm glad to hear it," Leona said warmly. "You seem like a good lad, Gareth. Is this what you signed up for? Malachai only needs the Tidecaller, after all. Surely it would be a simple matter to cast a forgetting spell over the rest of us and let us go on our way."

"It's not like that," Gareth said quickly. "Forgetting spells don't always work. Besides—"

"Then what *do* you think Malachai will do with us?"

Another lengthy pause met Leona's sharp words. With my magic, I could sense that Gareth's doubts were beginning to torture him.

"I'm sorry," he muttered. "This is just the way things are."

"Let's be honest with each other," I interjected. "We all know that Malachai will kill us after we're no longer useful to him—even me, if he finds a way to wield the powers of the amulet himself."

"Aye," said Leona. "But that isn't what you joined for, is it, Gareth?"

"No," he admitted sadly. "It isn't."

"I know exactly how you feel," said Isadora, sensing her opportunity to jump in. "Did you know that I was once under Malachai's sway?"

"You—you were?"

"Aye, friend. I was young and naive, disgusted with the brazen abuses of wealth and power that are all too common in this world. When Malachai shared his vision with me, I was convinced that he had a better way."

"So was I," Gareth said softly.

"Listen to me, Gareth. The course you're following leads only to darkness. But even though the current is strong, the crosswinds are stronger—provided you have the strength of will."

"'Strength of will'?" Gareth said bitterly. "What do you expect me to do? Rebel? Run away?"

"Aye," Isadora answered. "Join us, Gareth. Help us escape. Free yourself from Malachai's chains."

He paused, fidgeting uncomfortably. "You don't know what you're asking."

"Yes, I do," Isadora said firmly. "I once stood on the same side as you, lad. I know all the ways that Malachai keeps you bound to your fears."

"A life lived in fear is no life at all," Leona said fiercely. "I would rather risk my life than waste away in a dark sorcerer's thrall."

"Malachai's grasp reaches far," Gareth argued, though his words lacked conviction.

"Only as far as your fear," Isadora answered, her voice carrying the strength of someone who had broken free.

"Think of it, Gareth," I urged, pleading through the door's narrow bars. "Your skills are wasted here, serving a man whose thirst for power knows no bounds. With us, you could chart a new path. Join us, and make things right again."

The silence stretched like a taught bowstring. At length, Gareth let out a deep sigh.

"What's your plan?"

***

The flickering torchlight danced off the damp stone walls as Gareth returned, key in hand. He unlocked the heavy iron door, its creaking hinges echoing through the chamber. My heart began to race.

"Ready?" Gareth asked, his voice barely louder than a whisper. I glanced at Leona and Isadora, who nodded resolutely.

"Ready," I answered for all of us.

We filed out of the cell, moving catlike through the shadows. Gareth guided us through a maze of damp corridors that smelled of seaweed and brine. I tried not to think about the fact that the only thing keeping these tunnels from caving in was Malachai's dark magic.

"Where are we going?" Leona asked in a hushed voice.

"An old tunnel we sometimes use for smugglers," Gareth answered. "Malachai wants it kept sealed, but I managed to pry it open for us."

"Sounds risky," Isadora muttered as she scanned the darkness warily. "Are you sure Malachai isn't watching it?"

"Trust me," said Gareth, meeting her gaze.

The tunnel angled upward again, leaving the briny depths behind. Still, the air was thick with the pungent scent, as if it hadn't circulated properly in years.

"Hush," Gareth cautioned as footsteps sounded above. Just how large was this hideout anyways?

As the voices moved away and disappeared around a bend, Gareth lowered his torch and quickly put it out in the sand at his feet. We waited in silence for our eyes to adjust to the darkness. Only the light of distant torches met our eyes, barely enough to see by. Every shadow seemed to move, every creak of the timbers became a threatening harbinger of discovery.

"Stay close," Gareth whispered at length.

We followed him quietly around the next bend in the tunnel. Rats skittered ahead of us, making my heart leap. Their beady eyes seemed to glow in the darkness, sending chills down my spine.

As we went a little further, I suddenly realized that I could hear the ocean. I held my breath in an effort to contain my growing excitement. We were almost there—those crashing waves were the sound of our freedom.

"Not long now," Gareth whispered, pointing to sandy fissures in the roof above. Up ahead was a trapdoor, which he opened ever so slowly. After poking his head through, he came back down and nodded.

One by one, we climbed up the short ladder into the smuggler's cache. It was large and empty, with a sandy wooden floor and a pair of double doors lying at an angle in the ceiling, like the entrance to a cellar. Through the fissures in the planks, the moonlight shone through, as bright as a beacon in the near-total darkness.

"Is that the way out?" Leona asked.

"Yes," said Gareth. "Let's move. Quickly now."

He cracked the door open ever so slightly, sending a little cascade of sand into the cache. We dared not open the doors completely, but scrambled out one at a time as best we could. Gareth went first, Isadora taking the rear.

I have never been so happy to be under an open sky. After crawling through those dank, dark tunnels, all I wanted was to stand up straight and let out a whoop of triumph. But we kept our heads down as we moved among the beach grass, walking quickly but silently. This was, after all, the most dangerous part of our escape.

"There," said Gareth, motioning to a small, weather-worn boat. It had obviously lain there for some time, but between his magic and what little remained of mine, we could probably patch it up well enough to take us to the next island, where we could find a better means of transportation. Gareth had even had the foresight to stash some supplies nearby, including some much-needed food. We paused for a moment to eat, knowing that we would need our strength on the voyage ahead.

"Gareth," a voice suddenly sounded, so close it was nearly in our ears. "I thought I detected your treachery."

We leaped to our feet, but it was too late to run. Malachai emerged from the shadows of the trees, flanked on all sides by his followers. Within moments, they surrounded us.

"It's me you want, Malachai," I said, thinking quickly. "Let the others go."

"And betray the location of our base? I think not, Tidecaller."

The reconstructed amulet hung from his neck. Its smooth, dark face glinted in the flickering light of the cultists' torches. Though my magic was still weak, I could feel the dark stone calling to me, promising depths of power I had never known.

An idea suddenly came to me. Maybe our only chance.

I lunged forward, reaching for the amulet. A burning sensation spread across my scalp—after all, my magic was still only a fraction of what it used to be—but it was enough to tap into the power of the amulet. Malachai stepped back quickly, evading my grasp, but the amulet was still in sight. So long as that remained true, I could still wield at least a portion of its power.

The sudden flow of magic was like fire in my veins. Exerting all my might, I channeled it into my friends, enhancing their strength like never before. The cultists rushed them, but they leaped into the sea, swimming like fish for the next island over. As soon as they were in the water, I cast the deepest spell of concealment that I could concoct, and they vanished.

Malachai took the amulet in both hands, and my access to its power suddenly fled. I gasped and fell to the sandy beach, exhausted.

Why didn't I use my magic to save myself, you ask? To be honest, I'm not exactly sure. It could have been a basic heroic impulse. After all, splitting my attention between myself and my friends was liable to get us all killed. Or perhaps it was simply an act of cowardice, doubting that I had the power to save myself. But whatever it was, there was no time to think—only act. And in the end, it's our actions that define who we are, not the reasoning behind them.

"Fool," said Malachai, his voice dripping with contempt. "Had you come willingly, I would have kept them alive, even if only as tools to control you. But now, they shall all perish."

I answered by spitting in his face. Malachai cast a binding spell over me, and his followers stuffed me into a sack before beginning to beat me senseless with their staves. Beyond the pain, I don't remember much after that.

In Which I Face My Darkest Moment and Everything Comes to a Head

The windowless chamber was shrouded in eerie darkness. The only source of light was a single flickering candle, but it only seemed to enhance the shadows looming around the edges of the room. I sat on an ancient wooden chair, my arms tightly bound, atop a magic circle drawn in chalk on the floor. The rope chafed against my wrists and forearms, but no matter how much I struggled, I couldn't break free.

Malachai emerged from the shadows, gliding across the floor without a sound. In the dim light, his wicked smile glinted like a sharpened blade.

"Samuel," he purred, "you've been quite the slippery fish to catch. But now, you're finally mine."

I frowned, trying to muster some show of defiance. But in my weakened state, all I could manage was a pitiful glare. If my hair had not been shorn, perhaps I could have found a way to break my bonds. But even that was doubtful, considering the hold his magic had on me.

"You want this, don't you?" he said softly, producing the Tidecaller's Amulet. It seemed to call to me as it glistened in the flickering light.

I clenched my jaw. "You'll never break me, Malachai."

He smiled and let the pendant fall against his chest. "Break you? My dear Samuel, I have no need to break you. You're a broken man already."

"That's not true."

"You flatter yourself. I've had my eye on you for some time, even before you left the King's Fleet. You do remember that, don't you? The utter disgrace of it? Your life's first failure—the first of many."

I gritted my teeth, refusing to let his barbed words get to me. But as he continued to speak, I felt my resolve begin to weaken.

"Have you no retort?" he sneered cruelly. "No counterpoint? Of course not. We both know how much that broke you. If not for your friend Jason, you would never have become a sea mage. His pity was the only thing keeping you afloat all these years."

"You're a liar," I managed to choke out. "I know how to hold my own."

"Perhaps," said Malachai, fingering the amulet. "But until we met, you hardly knew anything about your true powers. In fact, you considered them more of a curse than a blessing, seeing as how they depended upon your hair. Even among sea mages, you always were something of an outcast—and that, too, was enough to break you."

The knot in my stomach tightened. His words were like poison, feeding my self-doubt. I squeezed my eyes shut, willing myself to find an anchor in the maelstrom of his words.

"Leona doesn't think so. Leona doesn't care what I do with my hair."

"The good Captain Black is an outcast herself. In giving her that letter of marque, King Leander is merely using her for his own purposes—exactly how I plan to use you. And I will, Samuel. Whether you are willing or not."

"Enough!" I shouted, my voice sounding hollow in the vastness of the shadowy room. "Your words are full of lies!"

"Are you so certain?" Malachai answered, his voice barely louder than a whisper. "The time is long past to keep squandering your gifts. Your so-called 'friends' are gone. No one is coming for you now."

I clenched my eyes shut and willed myself not to hear him. But my efforts were in vain as his voice hissed snake-like in my ear.

"Do you really think Jason would condescend to leave his wife and estate behind to come looking for you? No—he and Julietta are only fair-weather friends. As for Leona, she knows that there's nothing you can do to save her from me. She has no intention of coming back for you."

"She will!" I argued, but my words lacked conviction. Memories of my past failures flooded my mind, drowning out any hope or strength I had left. I could feel my resolve slipping away, replaced by a crushing despair.

"Give yourself over to me, Samuel," Malachai softly urged. "Your resistance is useless. Accept your fate and join me. Together, we can unlock the true potential of your power."

"Never," I growled.

Malachai grinned. "Stubborn to the end," he murmured, almost admiringly. "But if you will not do it for me, perhaps you will do it for her."

He turned, and Aurora's lithe figure stepped out of the shadows. My heart began to hammer against my ribs, each beat threatening to undo me. She bit her lip and gave me a sad look as Malachai loomed over the both of us.

"Please, Samuel," she said, her voice trembling. "Stop fighting. Malachai has already won—it's only a matter of time before he breaks you."

"No," I said, my anger flaring. "Just because—"

"Aurora is one of my truest followers," said Malachai, cutting me off. "Your failure to see that was your fatal flaw. And in the end, you will thank her for bringing you to me."

"Go to hell!" I spat in rage. Malachai's expression quickly cooled, but Aurora's face was a mask.

"You are a foolish man, Samuel," Malachai told me. "You carry yourself like a king, when in truth you are a fallen pawn, too weak to claim a single square. But no matter. In the fullness of time, you will accept your fate, willingly or no."

He turned and motioned for Aurora to join him. She hesitated a moment, her eyes meeting mine.

"I'm sorry, Samuel. I never wanted it to come to—"

"Come," said Malachai, his voice barely louder than a whisper. She stiffened and turned like a marionette at his command.

"Aurora!" I shouted as they vanished into the shadows. But she was gone, leaving me with only my doubts for company.

Everyone has a breaking point. Although I was prepared for physical torture, time can break down even the hardiest stone. I have no idea how long I sat there, bound atop the magic circle in that dank and windowless chamber. It could have been days. It could have been mere hours. My breath was the only sound to break the awful silence, itself another form of torture.

My thoughts tormented me almost as much as Malachai's words. Was I truly just a washed-up failure? No matter how hard I tried, I couldn't think of a single thing I'd done that hadn't ultimately come to naught. Even Julietta's rescue had been more due to Jason than to me. And Aurora—had she truly betrayed me? Or was Malachai right? Should I thank her for what she'd done to me?

All the while, I could feel the call of the amulet, even through the chamber's thick stone walls. Never had I felt so powerless, and the brief moment during the escape when I'd called upon its magic to strengthen my friends left me yearning to feel that power flow through me once again. And was this not the thing for which I had been born? To be the tide-caller—to have that kind of unimaginable power flow through me once again—

No. I shook my head and did my best to cast those tempting thoughts from out of my mind. But in the awful, empty silence of that darkened room, my thoughts were the only company I had left. It was only a matter of time before I succumbed.

Or was it?

A creaking door, a gentle draft, a shimmer of movement in the shadows. I lifted my groggy head and saw a familiar face in the flickering candlelight.

"Aurora?"

"Shh," she whispered, hastening to my bonds. "I've cast a spell to hide us, but Malachai's magic is stronger than mine. A loud word could break it."

For a moment, I was stunned. Had she come to rescue me? My mind began to clear as she cut me free from my bonds.

"Why are you doing this?" I asked, rubbing the soreness from my wrists.

"Because I love you," she whispered fiercely. "And because I've had a change of heart."

"But—why?"

She knelt and used her knife to cut the ropes around my ankles. "I'm sorry, Samuel. Malachai deceived me. I truly thought that bringing you here was the best thing I could do for you."

"And so, you betrayed me?" I hissed, blood rushing to my cheeks. "You cut my hair, Aurora. *You cut my hair!*"

"Shh! Not so loud. But yes, Sam—I hurt you and I betrayed you. Can you forgive me?"

I clenched my fists, but the rage soon fled from me. She was my sister, after all. Sighing heavily, I looked into her pleading eyes.

"We're family, Aurora. That means more than all of this. More than Malachai, more than the cult—"

"I know," she whispered. "Mother would have wanted you to be free."

"No. She would have wanted both of us to be free."

Aurora nodded and smiled as she cut through the last of my bonds. "You forgive me, then?"

"Only if you promise to leave this damned cult behind."

"Of course," she answered eagerly. "I can see through Malachai's lies now. I've been lost in the darkness long enough. You're right, Sam—family is everything."

She rose to her feet and embraced me. At that moment, Malachai's laughter suddenly filled the chamber. I spun, fists raised, as the dark sorcerer emerged from the shadows.

"So touching," he purred viciously. "But ultimately, so naive."

"Malachai!" Aurora gasped—but before she could say more, he lifted a single finger and his magic bound her tongue.

"Your usefulness has come to an end, girl. Had you not betrayed me, I would have given you a seat at my side. But now, you are naught but a failure—just like your brother."

"Leave her out of this!" I shouted. I rushed forward and threw a fist at Malachai's face. Normally, his wards should have been strong enough to stop me, but my eyes caught sight of the Tidecaller's Amulet hanging from his neck, and I instinctively drew upon its power. My fist connected with Malachai's jaw, sending him spinning to the floor.

In the sudden rush of magic from the amulet, my awareness expanded to the hallways and corridors beyond the darkened chamber. In that instant, I saw Leona and Isadora running toward us, aided by Gareth's and Aurora's spells. My heart leaped as I realized that Aurora had planned all of this—that she must have reached out to Gareth and found some way to sneak them back in before coming to free me. Everything she'd told me about leaving the cult behind was true.

"Fool!" Malachai shouted, rising swiftly to his feet. "I will make you pay for—"

"Leona!" I shouted—and in that moment, the door to the chamber burst open with a thunderous clang. Leona and Isadora both surged into the room, swords in hand and black and golden hair streaming behind them like battle flags. Gareth was not far behind.

"Sam!" Leona answered, putting herself between me and Malachai. "Stay close!"

An awful, screeching yell issued from Malachai's mouth, and an aura of dark power began to shimmer all around him. Leona and Isadora hesitated, and in that moment, another door opened, letting in a flood of cultists. They brandished their staves as they ran to their master's defense, quickly surrounding us.

"Keep your head down!" Isadora snapped, parrying a cultist's blow with her blade.

"Sam—the amulet!" Aurora shouted from behind me.

I looked and saw that Malachai was retreating, his hands outstretched as he called upon his magic to strengthen his men. The amulet hung on his chest, still tempting me with its power.

"We're with you, Sam!" Leona shouted as her sword sang through the air. Beside her, Gareth's staff cracked against bone, sending a cultist to the ground.

A storm of emotions surged within me—fear, anger, hope—but above all else, determination. I was done running, done being used as a pawn in Malachai's twisted game. And as I glanced from my sister to my friends, who had risked everything to save me, I knew what I had to do.

"Your reign ends here, Malachai!" I shouted, drawing upon my magic. It swelled within me like a tide ready to break free, and I focused it all upon him as I rushed forward, heedless of the arcane energy that surged all around me.

My hands grasped the amulet, and with all my strength, I wrenched it free. Malachai was so surprised by my sudden movement that he stumbled backward, blinking in surprise. Power surged within me as I held the amulet, whole and complete. Without Malachai's lies to blind me, I could crush him and his followers like bugs, free our friends, and then—

No, I told myself. The amulet had to be destroyed. To draw upon its full powers even for another instant was to fall prey to the same temptation that had led to the downfall of my people so many ages ago. It was not I who sought to wield the amulet, but the amulet that sought to wield me. If I gave in any more to it, all would ultimately be lost.

I fell to my knees, clutching the amulet with both hands as if to crush it. But though I called upon all the power that I possessed, the amulet refused to be destroyed.

Malachai's laughter cut through the chaos of the battle. "You think you can destroy this ancient artifact so easily?" he sneered, his voice like a serpent's hiss. "Fool! Even with your magic, you are nothing but a failure!"

"Sam!" Aurora shouted. I looked up just in time to see her toss me my scrimshaw locket. It sailed over the heads of the cultists, and in that moment, I suddenly remembered: my locket—my hair—

I snatched the locket and quickly opened it, spilling out the hair that my sister had shorn from me. Grasping a clump of it, I held it against the amulet, just as I'd seen in the vision from the compass. Malachai's eyes suddenly widened.

"Impossible!" he shouted as I called upon my power once again. The room spun with light, a torrent unleashed by the bond with my past, my heritage, my magic. The air crackled with energy, the very stones of the chamber humming as if to break asunder.

"By the locks of my ancestors!" I shouted.

Everything around me suddenly turned into a blur of light and energy. I heard—nay, felt—a scream of pure and primal rage, and realized with a start that it came not from Malachai but from the Tidecaller's Amulet itself. The amulet had deceived him as completely as he had deceived his own followers.

And then, it shattered into a thousand shards of light. A burst of power rent the air, disintegrating the remains of the amulet into a cloud of glittering dust and knocking me to the ground. My vision swam, and the light around me died as I passed out from the blow.

My ears still rang from the explosion as I pushed myself up from the cold stone floor. Through the haze of dust and debris, I saw the last of the cultists scramble into the labyrinthine corridors of their hideout. Malachai and his followers had gotten away, but without the Tidecaller's Amulet, they posed little threat to us now. They would not risk striking back at us when they did not know the disposition of our forces.

I shook the grit from my hair, feeling my magic slowly return. The heavy scent of expended magical energy hung like ozone in the air. My limbs ached, weariness tugging at my bones, but within my heart, the triumphant flames of victory burned bright.

It was over. The Tidecaller's Amulet was no more.

"Sam!" Leona called, her voice strained. She limped toward me, clutching her side where a fresh wound was bleeding through her tunic.

"Are you all right?" I asked, frowning in concern as I struggled to stand.

"Never better," she grinned. The light in her eyes remained unquenched, despite her injuries. Isadora and Gareth soon joined us, sword and stave in hand.

"That was quite an explosion, Sam," Isadora quipped. "I hope it was more than a parlor trick."

"It was," I assured her, holding up the pendant where the amulet had once been set. "The amulet has been destroyed."

"Thank the gods," she breathed as she gave me a grateful smile. Before I knew it, she had wrapped her arms around me in a fierce and happy embrace.

"Seems Malachai underestimated you," Leona said as Gareth helped bandage her wound.

"No," said Isadora. "He underestimated all of us."

"Are the cultists all gone?" I asked, glancing around the chamber. A part of me feared they would be back—this was their hideout, after all.

"Yes," came a voice from the shadows. A slender and long-haired figure stepped out—my sister, Aurora.

"Aurora," I said, embracing her warmly. She clung to me as if she would never let go.

"I'm so sorry, Sam," she bawled. "I never should have betrayed you. Malachai promised that fewer people would be hurt his way, but—"

"Hey," I said, wiping a tear from her eyes. "It all worked out in the end, didn't it? Thanks for being there when I needed you."

She smiled a little, then nodded. "I see you've regained at least some of your magic."

"It seems like I have," I said incredulously. Letting her go, I grinned and held up the scrimshaw locket where I had kept the lock of my hair. A few stray strands still clung to it, dark and frazzled.

"Did it help?" she asked. "In the middle of the fight, I suddenly had this thought that you needed it, but I didn't know why. What is it?"

"It's mother's old locket," I explained. "Our father gave it to me when I was young. After you cut my hair, I saved a lock of it inside, though I didn't know why at the time." I paused for a moment to think. "Seems like without it, I would have lost all my powers when the amulet was destroyed."

"But... you'll never be the mage you once were," she said softly. "And without the amulet... all that power... you'll never feel it again."

"I know," I said, feeling a pang at the loss. "But that doesn't matter so much. What matters now is family."

"Family indeed," said Leona. "And not just by blood."

"Agreed," Isadora responded.

"Besides," I added, running a hand through my shaggy locks. "I didn't lose *all* of my powers."

I summoned an orb of light that illuminated the chamber, chasing the shadows away. Though the ceiling above us was partially wrecked, with sand slowly pouring down from the beach above, the wards on the walls still held back the sea, and the rest of the hideout was more or less intact. All that was left of the cultists were a few scattered candles and the black-cloaked bodies of their dead.

"We should free our crew and get out of here," Isadora said quickly. "Before Malachai and the others come back."

"Aye," Leona agreed. "Gareth?"

"Come with me. I'll take you to them."

We fell into step behind him, Aurora and I lingering behind. "Can we really start over?" she asked, her voice tentative.

"Start over?" I said, taking her arm. "You're family, Aurora. That was just as true before as it is now."

She smiled, and for the first time ever, I sensed that her heart held no fear.

In Which I Settle Old Scores, Say Farewell, and Finally Sign on to a Ship

The cultists' hideout was impressive, I'll give them that. We saw barely a fraction of the winding, maze-like corridors that they'd built under the water-logged sand. Leona and Isadora kept their weapons drawn as they followed Gareth to the dungeon, while Aurora and I hung close behind.

"What are the odds that Malachai's set up an ambush for us?"

"That's not his style," she assured me. "It's more likely he'll just withdraw his magic and let the whole place collapse. This island is barely more than a sandbar, after all."

My eyes widened. "Hey guys, let's hurry it up!"

"This way," said Gareth, leading us to the dungeon. Sure enough, as we rounded the corner, we saw several large cells with dozens of men trapped inside: Leona's and Isadora's crews, all thrown in together.

"Hey Captain! Get us out of here!"

"Yeah! It's starting to leak!"

The men were suddenly all shouting at once, Gareth fumbling for the keys. I ran to the nearest lock and summoned my magic to break it. With my powers only a fraction of what they once were, it took a lot of concentration, but I managed to get it done.

"Up, up, up!" Aurora urged, directing the men to the stairs and up to freedom. Down the next corridor, the sound of rushing waters was growing disturbingly loud. I suddenly had the sense that we were trapped in a crumbling sandcastle as the tide was coming in.

I turned, expecting to find Leona and Isadora at each other's throats as they struggled to free their men. They both had strong personalities, after all, and until just a few days ago, they'd been bitter rivals. But to my amazement, they worked with practiced efficiency to break the locks and free all of the men, working much faster than either could have alone.

"Clear," said Isadora, bringing down the rock that she'd been using as a hammer on the improvised wedge that Leona had jammed into the keyhole. The old, rusted lock busted open, and Leona flung the door open while Isadora moved to the next one, already wedging the lock open.

"Up the stairs! Up the stairs!" Gareth and Aurora urged. "Move, move, move!"

Together, we freed all the men, breaking open the last cell just as the floors and walls began to collapse. It was close, but we got out to the surface just in time. Half of the island must have caved in behind us, leaving a massive watery sinkhole filled with all sorts of debris. But we were safe on the beach, with the *Ebony Eagle* and Isadora's ship both anchored a short distance away. Malachai's followers must have brought them in for salvage, then abandoned them in their hurry to leave the place.

"Good work," said Leona, turning to her erstwhile rival. "For a sea witch, you sure can move when the circumstances demand it."

"You're not so bad yourself," Isadora said with a wink. "Certainly faster than the last time. As I recall—"

"Ha! There'll be none of that, sister, lest I jog your memory of all the other times we've clashed blades."

"All right," said Isadora, extending her hand. "We'll call it a draw."

Leona grinned and shook, and the two captains embraced under the light of the moon. I couldn't help but smile at the sight of them.

"Uh, Captain?" Gareth asked, approaching Isadora. His eyes, once clouded with doubt, now shone with a newfound purpose.

"Yes, Gareth?"

"I... I would like to join your crew, if you'll have me. I wish to atone for my past mistakes."

She looked him over and gave him an approving nod. "I won't overlook your past misdeeds. But I know it takes courage to cast aside the mantle of a cultist."

"Then you'll have me?" Gareth asked.

"I'll give you a chance to prove your loyalty. Whether you find a place among us is up to you."

"Thank you," he murmured gratefully.

Meanwhile, Leona scowled as she examined her wounded ship. Moonlight bathed her decks in silver, but without her mainmast, there was no denying that she couldn't sail.

"Malachai must have towed her here with those damnable longboats of his," she muttered as Isadora walked over.

"Looks like your work is cut out for you, sister."

"Aye. But where shall we find a mast?"

"Look around," she said, gesturing to the flotsam drifting in the surf. "Between your mage and mine, I'm sure we can rig something together."

"I can help as well," said Gareth, eager to prove himself.

Aurora stepped forward. "Don't forget me!"

We worked together to fashion a new mast from the wreckage of the hideout. Isadora's ship mage was a burly islander named Tukuafu, whose magical powers lay in his intricate tattoos. He was surprisingly friendly once you got to know him, though he only spoke in pidgin. Combining his magic with mine and Gareth's, we were able to accomplish more than any one of us could have done alone, masterfully splicing the shattered pieces of debris into a workable mast. By the first light of dawn, the *Ebony Eagle* was repaired and ready to sail.

"Impressive," said Leona, walking around the deck to admire it. "I feared it would be ugly, but it looks like the *Eagle* has lost none of her charm."

"The charm of a bed of bones in a dragon's lair," Isadora smirked from beside her.

"Like I said. Charm."

"Tukuafu says she should hold until we get back to Caravelia," said Aurora. "Perhaps longer."

"Oh, I hope so," said Leona. "In fact, I hope to keep this mast for a very long time."

Isadora glanced over at her ship, where her men now awaited her and her mage. "I'm afraid this is where our headings must diverge," she said. "My men are eager to get back to Cole's Cove."

"Aye, and mine are just as ready to take their share of the reward from the king."

"Safe travels then, Captain Stone."

"And fair winds to you."

The two erstwhile rivals embraced before Isadora and her men climbed down to the waiting launch. As we watched them row back to their ship, I turned to Aurora.

"You're coming with us then?"

"If that's all right," Aurora said nervously.

"Of course!" said Leona. Then, turning to her men. "Don't just stand there, you sea dogs! Raise the anchor and unfurl the sails!"

The sun shone high in the sky as we approached the bustling port city of Caravelia. Saltwater mist rose from the sea, leaving a pleasant tang on my lips, and the wind carried the scent of fish and exotic spices through the air. The *Ebony Eagle* cut smoothly through the waves, her sails billowing as she took us all home.

"Feels good to be back, doesn't it?" Leona asked, standing on the deck beside me.

"Indeed," I agreed, feeling a warmth in my chest that had been absent for too long. We were returning as unsung heroes, but that was all right. We all knew the difference we'd made.

The winds blew fair, all the way to the docks in Caravelia's bustling harbor. As the men tied her fast and Leona issued orders, Aurora leaned against the railing beside me, her eyes distant as she gazed at the city beyond.

"So this is Caravelia," she said softly. "It's... beautiful."

"Just wait until you see the throne room," I told her, smiling as I pointed out the massive castle overlooking the bustling scene.

Leona walked over to us, a peacock's feather adorning her silk hat. "The ship is secure. Shall we go up to see the king?"

"The king?" Aurora asked, her eyes wide. My smile grew even broader.

Together, the three of us disembarked and climbed the steep cobblestone streets of the city. Aurora took my arm, staring in wonder at the vast crowds of city goers and the vibrant colors of the market stalls as the merchants peddled their wares. I held her close, feeling a fierce and brotherly protectiveness for her, but I needn't have worried—there was no threat to us here.

"You know," said Leona, "beyond the reward that King Leander is sure to give us, we aren't going to get much for this voyage. After all, no one sings your praises if you save them from a threat they can't see."

"That's all right," I told her. "True heroes need no accolades."

"Aye," said Leona, chuckling. "And pirates care for naught but the gold."

"Is King Leander expecting us?" Aurora asked.

"Aye," I answered, "so let's not keep him waiting."

The lavish opulence of the court made Aurora's eyes widen in awe, even as I was filled again with the sense that I was out of place. Vaulted ceilings loomed over us, and the halls echoed with the murmur of rich courtiers draped in velvet and silk. Heart suddenly pounding, I led the way, flanked by Aurora and Leona, whose presence lent me courage.

Just as we entered the great hall, an incredulous voice spoke my name.

"Samuel?"

I turned to find Soren's menacing eyes fixed on me with a vicious sneer. "I didn't think I'd see you again," he hissed.

"You thought wrong," I said, clenching my fists. "We have unfinished business, you and I."

"And what would that be?" he asked, feigning ignorance.

"Betrayal," I spat back at him.

He let out a mocking laugh. "Do you think anyone will believe the word of a scruffy, washed-up dropout over the word of a captain in the King's Fleet?"

"They will when I vouch for him," said Leona, stepping forward. Her eyes were deadly cold. "And they'll certainly believe me when I tell them how you ran off with the amulet."

"It's over, Soren," Aurora added. "Malachai's done. The cult has been scattered."

Soren's eyes suddenly flared in panic, then narrowed as he feigned ignorance again. "The 'cult'? Whatever are you talking about?"

"Cut the crap, pretty boy," Leona snapped at him. "We all know you were in league with Malachai. You were part of his cult all along."

"And what proof do you have? It's the word of a thieving pirate against mine!"

"And mine," said Aurora. "I was in the cult, too, Soren. My testimony alone is sufficient to bring you down."

For a moment, Soren just stared at her. Then, like a viper suddenly striking from the dust, his sword leaped into his hand.

"Aurora!"

I lunged out to shield her with my body just as Leona's blade knocked Soren's aside. He lashed out viciously, but she parried his blows with ease, sending a riposte that slashed his cheek. He howled and stumbled backwards in pain.

The guards rushed toward us as a shout went up from the other courtiers. Leona held up her hands as they took her sword, but the guards had to pry Soren's from his hands.

"Traitors!" he shouted for all to hear. "They—they're traitors to the crown!"

"Liar!" I shouted back frantically. "Soren is the traitor—he betrayed us and left us to die!"

"That's right," Aurora added, hugging my arm.

"What is the meaning of this?"

King Leander's mighty voice echoed through the chamber as he stalked forward, his ermine robes flowing in his wake. I fell immediately to one knee, and Aurora and Leona quickly followed suit.

"Your Majesty," I said meekly. "Captain Black and I have returned with your commission to find and destroy the Tidecaller's Amulet."

"And?" he asked, his gaze unyielding.

"And our mission was a success," I answered. "The amulet has been destroyed, and it will pose a threat to your kingdom no more. But this man," I added, pointing to Soren, "betrayed us in the worst possible way."

"Lies, Your Majesty!" Soren sneered. "Samuel is the traitor, not I. He's lying about the amulet—he probably intends to use it against you as soon as he takes the reward."

"You slimy little snake!" Leona spat contemptuously. "It was you who stole the amulet from us and left us for dead!"

"Never, Your Majesty. As I told you before in my report, they—"

"Silence!" King Leander bellowed, raising his hands. "Who is this?" he asked, turning to my sister.

"Your Majesty, may I present my sister, Aurora."

"Your sister?"

"Yes," I told him. "She once was part of Malachai's cult but has since left them. Without her timely help, we would not have won the day."

"Your Majesty," she said, bowing deeply.

"Rise, my child," he commanded her. "What can you tell me about this affair?"

She hesitated, but only for a moment. "Your Majesty, I was indeed a member of Malachai's secret society, as my brother has explained. But Samuel helped me to see through his lies. He brought me back to the light."

"And the captain?" the king asked.

Aurora turned her gaze to Soren, whose eyes suddenly widened. "He is indeed a follower of the dark sorcerer, Your Majesty," she testified. "In fact, he is one of Malachai's chief lieutenants."

A gasp went up from the courtiers, who had surrounded us all by now. Soren opened his mouth to deny it, but King Leander silenced him with a gesture of his hand.

"Captain Black, what have you to say about all this?"

"Your Majesty," she said, bowing with a flourish. "Soren was the first to draw his sword today. Does that not testify against him?"

"Indeed, it does," said King Leander. Then, to the guards, he added, "Bind the traitor and throw him in the dungeon!"

"Your Majesty!" Soren squealed, his sneer turning to a look of utter desperation. But his cries were in vain, and the guards hauled him off like the piece of garbage he was.

By now, the court was buzzing with shock and excitement. A large and curious crowd had gathered to see the commotion. Among them I recognized Jason and Julietta.

"My apologies," said King Leander. "And thank you for helping me root out this traitor in our midst."

"Of course, Your Majesty," Leona and I both answered.

He smiled, his anger dissipating. "Come now. I want to hear a full report from each of you. It sounds like you've had quite an adventure."

Aurora took my arm again, and I glanced over my shoulder at Lady Julietta, who offered an encouraging smile. The courtiers all listened with rapt attention, and for the first time, I didn't feel so out of place in the king's court.

Later in the evening, after the sun had set, I stepped into the royal gardens in the castle courtyard. The stars were just beginning to pierce the twilight sky, and the scent of roses hung in the warm summer air. In a quiet, secluded spot along the path, my sister Aurora sat on a stone bench.

"Samuel," she said softly, her eyes meeting mine. Her voice was almost lost amidst the rustling of the leaves in the evening breeze, yet her presence in the garden was like an anchor to me.

"Aurora," I said, taking a seat beside her. "Thinking about the future?"

"Just like you, I imagine. You're free now, Samuel—free of the amulet, free of your hair's binding. Your magic is yours now, whether or not you choose to cut your hair."

"True," I mused, running my fingers through my shaggy locks. "But I think I'll keep it anyway, as a reminder of who I am and what I've been through." I paused, studying her reaction. "What do you think?"

She smiled. "I like it. Your hair has always distinguished you, just like your loyalty and resilience. I can understand why you would want to keep it."

I let out a long breath. "Thank you, Aurora."

We sat for some time in companionable silence, admiring the gardens and the shimmering light of the stars.

"I suppose our paths must diverge soon," Aurora said softly. "I want to spend some time catching up with our father, but you probably want to get back to sea."

"Yes," I answered. "But we'll see each other again."

"Of course we will. It's just... before you go, I wanted to know that you're my hero." She waved her hand, as if to indicate the city outside. "The rest of the world may never realize what you've done for them by destroying that cursed amulet, but I will never forget what you've done for me."

"Unsung heroes," I mused.

"As you said, true heroes need no accolades."

I nodded. Aurora put her hand on my arm.

"Wherever your journey takes you, Samuel, know that I will be forever grateful—not just for what you've done for me, but for who and what you are."

"Of course," I said, grinning. "After all, that's what family's for, isn't it?"

"I suppose."

We embraced warmly as brother and sister. But I've never been one for lengthy, drawn-out goodbyes, so I let her go and rose to my feet.

"Until we meet again."

"Yes," she whispered. "Until then."

I smiled and turned again to the meandering path. She resumed her seat on the stone bench, giving me a final wave.

As I left the garden and passed out of the castle, my thoughts turned to the next chapter of my life. I made my way down Caravelia's narrow cobblestone streets to the harbor, where the *Ebony Eagle* awaited.

"Samuel," Leona called to me. "Ready to make it official?"

"Aye," I told her, ascending the gangplank with a sense of renewed purpose. Far from being a castaway of fate, now I was its master, charting my own course through the waters of life.

We retired to her cabin, where she unfurled the voyage contract, written on a yellowed sheet of parchment. "As our sea mage," she explained, "you're entitled to two shares of the profit, along with the captain and quartermaster. Unlike the captain and quartermaster, however, you cannot be deposed by a majority vote of the crew."

"Why is that?" I asked.

"To ensure loyalty. After all, the rest of us are free to leave at any time, but a mage who jumps ship is liable to gain a reputation that can end his career. So much of our success depends on your abilities that it only makes sense that you should depend on us.

"I see. And we sign a contract like this for every voyage?"

"Aye," she said, nodding. "It's the pirate way. Though after all we've been through, I have no doubt that we'll be signing you on for many more voyages to come."

The pen was fashioned from a peacock's feather. I took it eagerly and signed my name, sealing my place among the crew.

"Welcome aboard, Sam," Leona said as she rolled up the parchment with a flourish. "Now get some rest—we sail at first light. The seas await!"

"Indeed," I said with a smile. "May the winds ever blow fair."

She grinned and shook my hand. "With you are our sea mage, I have no doubt that they will."

Author's Note

My goal in writing the Sea Mage cycle was to learn how to incorporate generative AI into my creative process and to practice my AI-assisted writing skills. If some of the books feel a bit rough, it's probably because of how I was reworking my writing process from the ground up. I didn't finish all of my Sea Mage Cycle books—in fact, just before writing *The Call of the Tide,* I trunked a novel attempt that had gone sideways. So in an effort to get the series back on track, I decided to write a direct sequel to the first Sea Mage book, *Rescuer's Reward.*

(Interestingly enough, *Rescuer's Reward* is not actually the first Sea Mage book that I tried to write. That one was a novel with the working title *Bloodfire Legacy,* which I started immediately after finishing my first AI-assisted novel, a fantasy standalone titled *The Riches of Xulthar.* But I wrote *The Riches of Xulthar* without using any of Sudowrite's Story Engine tools, so *Bloodfire Legacy* was my first attempt using those, which was probably why it fell apart. However, a lot of the characters in my other Sea

Mage books, like Seraph from *The Widow's Child* and Lady Callidor from *Rescuer's Reward* were originally in *Bloodfire Legacy,* so I will probably go back and rewrite that book at some point. It's got a pretty solid story arc.)

I started *The Call of the Tide* in January 2024, eager to get back into writing after the holidays (Christmas is fun, but it can also be a lot of work when you've got small children). My goals with the project were to experiment with first person, since that seemed to work out well with *The Winds of Desolation* and the other WIP that I hadn't yet trunked, and to just have a lot of fun. As with the other Sea Mage books, I jumped right into this one without doing a whole lot of prewriting or outlining. Mostly, I just threw all of my ideas into the story prompts and waited to see what the AI gave me.

In working with generative AI and large language models, I've come to realize that these AI tools can't actually think or use logic. Rather, they analyze the patterns of our language to create an imitation of something that a human would actually write. Sometimes it's a very good imitation, and other times it's a terrible imitation. Therefore, in planning out a story with AI, I've found that it's helpful to create a feedback loop between myself and the AI. I'll prompt the AI using some of my ideas, then take what the AI gives me and structure it into a story. For example, when writing the scene where Samuel dives into the shipwreck, I started out by prompting the AI that the amulet is in four pieces and to outline a different chapter where he finds each one. Then, after reviewing what the AI came up with, I thought it might be cool to put the first fragment in a shipwreck, and to use his magic to dive down and get it. Then, when coming up with the prompts for that chapter, I took the first couple of iterations and adjusted the beats to play up the best parts, generating new iterations of the chapter and using the AI tools to make those passages more descriptive or more intense.

This was the first AI-assisted project where I generated multiple iterations of each chapter, cutting and pasting the best parts from each one. It worked surprisingly well, to the point where this is now the standard method that I use whenever I write. I adopted this method originally in an effort to save credits, when Sudowrite switched from a pay-by-the-word model to a pay-by-the-credit model. The engine that I had been using was the most resource-expensive one, so I thought that I might be able to save some money by using a slightly less powerful engine, which was more likely to go off on random tangents, and copy-paste the good parts where the engine didn't stray too far from my original vision. But it turns out that using the same exact prompts for the same exact engine will still produce different texts every time, and that some of them will be better in parts than others.

After finishing the AI draft and moving on to the human draft, one of my goals was to hit 10k human words in a single day. This was not something I had ever achieved before, though I'd come close in some of my previous AI-assisted writing attempts. Years ago, Rachel Aaron wrote a writing book called *2k to*

10k, and this was really the genesis of that goal. I've never really felt that I was a very fast writer, so by hitting 10k words, I hoped to experience something of a breakthrough by proving to myself that these limiting beliefs weren't true.

So for the entire month of February, I pushed really hard to hit at least one 10k writing day, rereading Rachel Aaron's excellent book and restructuring my daily routine to make it possible. And at the very end of the month, I managed to hit it... and spent the next month or so feeling pretty burnt out. Yes, I did prove to myself that I could accomplish such a difficult goal, especially with the help of these AI writign tools, but I also relearned the importance of doing things to refill the creative well. Fortunately, the burnout wasn't permanent, and I was soon back to writing.

As of right now, I don't have any other Sea Mage books in the publishing queue. When I decided to republish them under my main pen name, I also decided to work on other projects, taking what I'd learned from practicing AI-assisted writing with these books. My next project after this one was *Captive of the Falconstar,* the second book in my (currently) unfinished Falconstar Trilogy, and after that I decided to work on short stories for a while. If there's sufficient reader interest, I may write some more books in this series, but for now I'm moving on to other things, though I would really like to revisit *Bloodfire Legacy* at some point, maybe even later this year.

If you enjoyed this book, please take the time to rate it or post a review. It really does help other readers to find it, and it also lets me know if I should write more books like it. To follow my writing and be updated whenever I have a new book, be sure to sign up for my email list. You can also check out my blog, One Thousand and One Parsecs, or send me an email at jvasicek.author@gmail.com.

That's all for now. Until next time, thanks for reading!

Joe
July 2024
HTTL

Acknowledgments

A big thanks to my writing group: Jeffrey Creer, Carl Duzett, Darci Stone, and Piper Vasicek. Thanks also to my editor, Josh Leavitt, my cover artist James, and my friend and sometimes co-writer Scott Bascom. Finally, I owe a huge thanks to my wife Piper, for all of her love and support, and for letting me dedicate this book to her. Love you!

www.ingramcontent.com/pod-product-compliance
Lightning Source LLC
LaVergne TN
LVHW010550160826
845677LV00013B/3066
* 9 7 9 8 2 3 0 5 9 7 5 5 1 *